# Praise for *I BRAKE FOR M*

Geeta Kothari's debut collection, *I Brake for Moose and Other Stories*, is a splendidly satisfying example of the possibilities peculiar to the liar's art, for hers are worlds—eleven of them between these covers—at once achingly real and deeply imagined, where we find only and always ourselves in masquerade: divided by impossible dreams, deracinated by war and want, and, in the end, made desperate by all the promises others have failed to keep. Ms. Kothari is that writer, out of so many deserving your attention, that again and again you will return to, keen to learn anew what magic, both dark and light, the willed word can make.

> – Lee K. Abbott, *All Things, All at Once: New and Selected Stories*

There are many ways to leave home...Geeta Kothari is here to tell us, and the tricky road back is always charged and uncertain. These stories chart that journey with aching accuracy.

> – Ron Carlson, author of *Return to Oakpine* and *A Kind of Flying: Selected Stories*

Stories can sometimes feel small, artificially sealed off from the tangled world we live in. Not these. These characters struggle movingly, often humorously, with difference: difference from the people around them, or from who their families once assumed they'd become, or from the futures and selves they once envisioned. Geeta Kothari is unafraid to explore both the complexities of identity, and the fears and frustrations of individual human hearts.

> – Caitlin Horrocks, author of *This is Not Your City*

These unusually varied stories are informed by Geeta Kothari's brilliant, and far-ranging imagination, so you never know what you're getting into. Every story is a new occasion, a new land, a new investigation into the identity of characters from all over the world, and a reminder that this formal and thematic dexterity is part of what informs, and makes necessary, the short story. Few collections take advantage of the form the way Kothari does here. The stories are imbued with her distinctly trenchant humor and wisdom, along with a quiet compassion for the grieving, the bewildered, and the misfit. Let's all hope this is the first of many collections from Geeta Kothari.

– Jane McCafferty, author of *First You Try Everything*

Long familiar with her stories, essays, and nonfiction, the legion of Geeta's fans have been anxiously awaiting this book that announces her incredible gifts to the world. The stories showcase a diversity that refuses to be pigeonholed, a political edginess always contained in its vulnerable human form, and an empathy too wired for a single current. A beautiful collection.

– Nancy Zafris, author of *The Home Jar*

I Brake for Moose and Other Stories

# I BRAKE FOR MOOSE

## and Other Stories

by Geeta Kothari

BRADDOCK AVENUE BOOKS

UNCOMMON BOOKS · UNCOMMON READERS

*Printed in the United States of America*
10 9 8 7 6 5 4 3 2 1

FIRST EDITION, February 2017

ISBN 10: 0-692-83000-0
ISBN 13: 978-0-692-83000-0

The following stories have appeared elsewhere in slightly different form: "Dharma Farm" and "Small Bang Only" in *Great Jones Street*; "Flight Attendants Take Your Seats" in *Weave*; "Border Crossing" appeared as "Ten Years Gone" in *Border Crossing*; "Waterville" in *Bananafish*; "Missing Men" in *Kenyon Review*; "I Brake for Moose" in *Massachusetts Review*; "Home is Another Country on TV" in *Rampike*; "The Spaces Between Stars" in *Her Mother's Ashes 2: More Stories by South Asian Women in Canada and the United States*, edited by Nurjehan Aziz; "Her Mother's Ashes" in *Toronto South Asian Review*; "Foreign Relations" appeared as "Meena's Curse" in *Screaming Monkeys: Critiques of Asian American Images*, edited by M. Evelina Galang.

*Book design and cover by Savannah Adams*

Alleyway Books
an imprint of
Braddock Avenue Books
P.O. Box 502
Braddock, PA 15104

www.braddockavenuebooks.com

Braddock Avenue Books is distributed by Small Press Distribution.

For Mark

# CONTENTS

# I BRAKE FOR MOOSE

## and Other Stories

# The Spaces Between Stars

Watching the fish squirm in Evan's gloved hands, Maya was transfixed by the fish's suffering. It had stopped moving for a second, but now it was struggling, its tail flapping back and forth, as it twisted for freedom, unaware that the hook lodged deep in its gut wouldn't let go.

"It's dying," she said. "We should have pushed down the barbs like that woman in the store told us to."

Evan grunted and peered inside the fish's mouth.

"I know what I'm doing."

Maya knew he was determined to give her a genuine, all-American fishing trip, the kind he used to go on when he was a boy outdoors, and she was a girl indoors, watching TV. Long before Evan, there had been a boy on TV, a boy with long lanky hair that hung across one eye. He had flicked it back impatiently as he baited his hook, explaining to the camera that the "crick" was his favorite place. She remembered that word "crick" because some of the kids at school said it, kids who were unaware of her but whom she observed from a distance.

The small sunfish, a swath of green and gold, glistened in Evan's hand. The sun beat down on the top of Maya's head, searing her scalp. She felt dizzy and a wave of sadness passed over her as she stared at the helpless fish.

"It's dying."

Evan gently placed the sunfish in the water and cut the line. It swam off, seemingly recovered from its near-death experience.

To cook the fish he had caught, the boy on TV dug up some fresh clay, patted it into two flat rounds, stuck the fish between them and baked it in the flames of his campfire. In her dreams, Maya would camp by that crick, fish and swim in it and sleep in a tent under the stars. How she would see the stars above her head while sleeping in a tent, she wasn't sure, but even in her fantasy life, she could not see herself sleeping without shelter.

Maya climbed back into the boat. Her line had been cut, and her mission had been achieved. She proved herself able to catch a fish, and now she wanted to go home. She handed Evan a turkey sandwich and looked over the side of the boat. Her fish, red at the gills, eyes bulging, floated towards them.

"Look," she said. "It died anyway."

Evan shrugged. "It was just a sunfish. They're everywhere."

Her guilt pressed against her temples, tightening like a vise around her head. Still she said nothing. She'd been the one who not only agreed but had been excited about going fishing. It had been one of the many activities forbidden to her during childhood. The expedition should have made her feel closer to Evan. Instead, Maya felt as if the parched brown hills surrounding the lake had sprung up between them. The inside of her skin itched, and she wanted to jump out of it, leave behind her body and the pervasive smell of dead fish.

She watched Evan eat his sandwich, oblivious to her inner turmoil as he basked in the sun. He was like that boy on TV. He was resourceful, knew how to do things that were beyond her realm of experience. He could pitch a tent, start a camp-fire, handle raw meat without feeling sick, open the hood of a car and see things. He could talk to strangers and get his way. Evan assumed he had the right number until told otherwise; he assumed cooperation and satisfaction, even when talking to the phone company about a bill. Making calls from one of her temporary jobs, Maya would begin her sentences with "I'm not sure..." and end them breathless, gasping for air, as she struggled to find the right words. Eventually, passed from one person to the next, trying to make herself understood, she would give up and leave the task for the next day. What looked like procrastination was something she couldn't begin to explain.

She had wanted to be that boy on TV, but what such boys were seemed hereditary, increasingly out of reach and unat-tainable. Instead, she forced herself through college and one dismal semester of graduate school. Then she married Evan.

They got home late in the afternoon, just as the thunder started rolling in. Evan shut himself up in his study while Maya napped. The heat had exhausted her, leaving her empty and dry inside.

Later, she made dinner, though she had no appetite or enthusiasm for the aloo gobi and dal. Nothing smelled or tasted right; the potatoes and cauliflower were mushy and the dal had too much cumin. Her shoulders felt sore from the sun, and the smell of fish lingered on her fingers. She rubbed her fingers with lemon juice until her cuticles burned, and still they smelled.

Evan padded into the kitchen, his blond hair sticking up as if he'd been sleeping and pulled a beer out of the refrigerator.

"Indian food. What's the occasion?" He leaned against the counter and stretched his legs across the narrow passage. Everything about him was long, lean and graceful. Next to him, she felt like a baby elephant—small, dark, and clumsy.

"None. Should there be?"

"You never make it, that's all."

"That's because I can't." Her voice got tighter, and she felt a rush of anger, making her face hotter above the steaming pots.

But Evan would not be drawn into a fight. "Don't forget, my folks are coming next week. And they want an answer about the trip."

Maya's stomach dropped. She'd forgotten both the ski trip at Christmas and the Everett's impending visit. Fortunately, the Everetts would stay with friends, as they always did. Though they'd never said anything, Maya sensed that she didn't keep house up to their standards. The brass incense holder, the small footstool inlaid with ivory, the embroidered mirror-work cushions, and the orange and red batik wall hangings had been passed on to her by her aunt, Shyamma. They seemed to go well with the reupholstered couch and chair from Evan's parents, but she was sure they didn't find the same comfort in this mixed decor.

Maya turned off the rice. When she looked up, she noticed that Evan was still in the room, watching her as she moved from stove to sink, counter to kitchen table.

"Are you all right?" he asked.

"Fine." He was the psychologist, she thought. Let him figure it out.

"Really?" He came over and kissed the back of her neck while she fluffed the rice. The individual grains had lost their definition and clung together, exactly what the recipe warned against.

"Allergies," she said, shrugging him off. Her long dark hair was coming out of its elastic band, sticking to the back of her sweaty neck. His lips against her skin reminded her of the fish, gasping for breath.

She couldn't tell him. She couldn't admit her failure in the great American outdoors. It was simply beyond her, to find the words for this thing she couldn't understand.

After dinner, Shyamma called.

First, she complained about the weather.

"Yesterday, I forgot to drink even one glass of water. Can you imagine? I nearly fainted in the kitchen."

"You have to pay attention, auntie." Maya could not call her Shyamma, the way Evan did, not out loud, even though Shyamma had told her to. "The heat isn't your friend, just because you don't like the cold."

Three, four times a week, Shyamma would call with a muted crisis or a question that needed an immediate response. A response, not an answer, Maya finally understood, and she listened, for Shyamma was the only family she had.

"And how is your dear husband?"

"Fine. He's nearly finished." Evan was working on his dissertation, and it gave Shyamma great pleasure to finally have a Ph.D. in the family. Evan's success made up nicely for the brilliant failure of Maya's academic career.

Maya wondered what Shyamma would say about her aborted conversion into a fisherwoman and her complicity in the death of the sunfish. What was okay for an Everett might be unacceptable for a Sohni. Shyamma was still a vegetarian. She prayed to her blue-faced gods and goddesses, and every day at sunset, burnt sweet grass and sage on a small piece of charcoal, carrying it reverently from room to room in the small house Maya had grown up in.

Shyamma asked about the Everetts, their two daughters, and everyone else under the Everett sun.

"Such a nice family," she sighed.

"Because they invite you to their stupid Christmas party?" Maya chewed a hangnail, enjoying the sharp pain that ran through her finger.

"Yes. And they always send me cards—Halloween, Easter, Christmas."

Holidays Shyamma used to dismiss as "Christian" or "American," having nothing to do with them. Not even a Christmas tree, Maya thought, and now she eats cookies shaped like Santa Claus and sings "Away in a Manger" without hesitation. After five years, she knew the words by heart, just like everyone else at the party.

"And so," Shyamma finally said. "How are you?"

"Fine. We went fishing today."

"That's nice bacchi."

Maya listened to the pots and pan clattering in the background. She doubted her aunt had heard her. Their conversation was over.

Shyamma had raised Maya alone, after her parents were killed in a plane crash. Rather than send Maya back to live with her paternal grandparents, Shyamma insisted on keeping her in the States. She herself didn't want to go back to India and marry the demented distant cousin her father had found for her.

"Understand," Shyamma once said, "I had a fellowship, and I was finally free. And I was afraid if I sent you to your father's people, we'd never see you."

They had been lonely in Erie, Pennsylvania. They knew no other Indian families with children. Most of Shyamma's friends were single women who worked full-time. She seemed not to miss her family whom they saw on rare visits to Delhi. Now, though, her loneliness had caught up with her. Maya heard it in the phone calls, the unasked "When are you next coming up?" During those cold, dreary winters, when the wind blew hard off the lake and kept them inside, Shyamma would tell Maya what a great life they had, how easy it was to be American, how good this country had been to her. But for Maya, growing up in a strict vegetarian household in Erie during the sixties was not fun. Shyamma banned Oreos because they were made with lard. At barbecues and school picnics, Maya hid her plate, heavy with potato salad, corn on the cob, coleslaw and an empty hot dog bun. Shyamma saw that Maya ate nutritionally sound meals, overlooking the conflict between this and Maya's sole desire: to be like everyone else and not like her aunt, who still lived in the culture she'd left over thirty years ago.

On their last trip to Erie, Maya and Evan had found Shyamma chilled and sick with the flu. She had hid it from them, she said, because she was afraid they wouldn't come up. The walk at Presque Isle, promised to Evan, was put off; it was too cold, even if they were healthy, Shyamma insisted. They spent the whole weekend indoors. Evan paced the small living room and stared out the window the way Maya used to when she was a child. Shyamma lay on the couch, reading magazines and marking all the things she would someday buy, when she had enough money. Her salary from the hospital was never quite enough; she was a woman with foreign syntax and got paid less than any man in the same position.

Such was Shyamma's freedom.

Later, in bed, Evan asked Maya again about the ski trip. His parents wanted to take them to Banff at Christmas, where a friend of theirs would let them stay for free.

"I don't think so."

Evan sat up and looked at her. Maya kept her eyes focused on her book and remained slouched against the headboard.

"You always said you wanted—"

"I'm too old. Why don't you go without me?"

Evan ran his hand through his hair. He looked at her for a minute and then got out of bed.

"Fine. You figure out a way to tell my parents why you're not coming."

Evan, Maya had learned a long time ago, was uninterested in confrontation, in talking things through. He left the room, and she heard him go into his study. He would work for the next few hours, slip into bed after she'd fallen asleep, and dream through the conflict. The next morning, he'd act as if nothing had been said, and by evening he'd be asking her the same question again. And if she did not give him the answer he wanted, the whole scene would repeat itself, day after day, until one of them—usually Maya—gave in.

She woke up early the next morning. Next to her, Evan slept soundly. Maya pushed his thin hair off his face and traced the outline of his ear, half willing him to wake up. He turned over to his other side, pulling the sheet with him. When she slid out of bed, he didn't move.

Down in the kitchen, watching the sky get lighter over the river, she smelled it, the dead fish smell. She sniffed the carton of cream, her fingers, the tail of her long braid. She opened the refrigerator, scanning the shelves for any forgotten beans, unwrapped meat or cheese. She pulled open the vegetable bin, checking for wilted broccoli, mushy tomatoes, and soggy lettuce. She threw out some moldy cottage cheese and a dried up piece of fudge cake.

Maya's feet stuck to the kitchen floor as she scrubbed the cabinet doors.

"You are so ungrateful," Shyamma used to say, when Maya was sixteen and came home at two in the morning, smelling of alcohol and back seat sex.

Maya shrugged. It didn't matter what she did, Shyamma would be there. They were family, blood in a world of strangers. Like fish, they swam in the same school, a school of two, but a school nonetheless, dodging predators, careful of false bait.

Maya had finally bitten. Life with Evan was too tempting, an easy guarantee that she would not end up like Shyamma. But the ski trip weighed on her, pulling her in a direction she wasn't sure she wanted to go. Evan's parents had welcomed her as easily as they welcomed Shyamma; now she wished for a little resistance, a disapproving arched eyebrow or a look of confusion when they saw her living room. Instead, Pat had smiled into the tiny mirrors, and Evy nodded as he eased himself in his old chair. She and Shyamma had done everything to make themselves acceptable, so why should the mixed decor worry the Everetts?

Maya brushed her teeth until her gums bled and the brush hurt her cheek. Once on a bus she saw a man scratching his arms with a steel comb, running it up and down along his forearm, until the skin was raised in thin red welts that looked ready to burst.

"Heroin addict," Shyamma said, after the man stumbled off the bus.

"How do you know?"

"When they need a fix, they itch so bad, they want to jump out of their skin. That was him."

Looking at her reflection in the bathroom mirror, Maya felt the same way. She wanted out of this skin, out of this life and into another, one that fit her, not one that she had to fit.

That night, when Evan asked again, Maya said, "I don't want to go."

She lay in bed, flat on her back. Light from the house next door cut through the open blinds, striping the rumpled cotton sheets. She stared at the ceiling, searching for the fluorescent stars Evan had pasted on it when they first moved in.

Evan rolled over on his side, facing her. "If it's the money—"

"It's not the money."

"Then what is it?"

Maya flopped over, turning her back to him. "When I was a kid, all I ever wanted was to go on our school ski trips. Every year they had one, and all the cool people went. Those who couldn't afford it did cross-country on their own. Shyamma wouldn't even let me do that. When I said she didn't trust me to take care of myself, she said it was too cold for me. She really meant it was too cold for her."

"So here's your chance," Evan said.

"I don't care anymore. I can't do it."

"You won't even try."

She turned to face him. In the dark, she couldn't read his expression, but she resisted the urge to turn the light on.

"Why is it so important that I ski?"

Evan sighed. "You're part of the family."

"Ralph doesn't ski. He's still part of the family, isn't he?" Evan's older brother-in-law refused to put on skis for political and economic reasons that the entire family teased him about.

"He's just scared."

"So? I bet Anne isn't forcing him to go to Banff."

"For God's sake." Evan punched his pillow. "You're the one who wanted to go fishing, you wanted to ski, and now you're blaming me." He left the room, slamming the door behind him, and then he slammed his study door as well.

Maybe she was scared. What if she couldn't really be an Everett? She was still horrified by her participation in the death of another creature. It was all very well to kill a fish on television or buy it at the store, nicely cleaned and filleted, but this—this was the beginning of a cycle she'd never be able to escape.

But what was the alternative? Maya lay on her back. On the ceiling, the stars glowed. There was the Big Dipper, the Little Dipper, Orion, the archer. Evan had followed the instructions so precisely, the whole sky filled their ceiling. When she initially suggested it, she'd thought of scattering them where she pleased. While she was out one day, Evan put them up, arranging each and every one just so.

When she showed her surprise, he frowned and said, "But that's how they're supposed to be. Every star in its place."

And where was hers? She had thought with Evan she would find it. But only if she forgot where she'd been before, and now she found that forgetting incomplete.

The next morning, Maya woke up at dawn and was on the road before the sun had completely risen. She didn't want to give herself the chance to change her mind and seeing Evan would have done that. She drove north on 79, past Mars, Moon Township, and the shrine in the median at Zelienople. A marker for someone who had died on the road, the small fir tree decorated for July 4th—red, white, and blue tinsel draped over it and an American flag languidly moving in the slipstream of the big trucks that roared by. At Easter, pastel-colored plastic eggs hung from its branches, and at Christmas someone garnished it with bright ornaments, including a gold angel for the top.

By the time she pulled into Shyamma's neat little driveway, with the marigolds lined up on either side, it was well past eight. She knew that Shyamma would be in the kitchen. Maybe she could talk her into making some masala chai, something to wash her mouth of the terrible gas station coffee she'd had an hour ago in Meadville.

Shyamma didn't look up from the counter where she was rolling out some dough.

"Evan called. He wants to know if you'll be home for dinner."

Her tone was accusing, on Evan's behalf.

"What are you making?" It could have been chapatti; it could have been poori. Maya didn't know.

Shyamma tucked a strand of hair behind her ear. Her hair was still black and shiny, a testament to the coconut oil she used regularly and rigorous brushing. Her small brown face was slack at the jaw and under the chin, but her cheeks were high and firm, turning into small apples when she smiled. She had a sweet smile, Evan said, like Maya. But neither of them was smiling now.

"Paratha." Shyamma kept rolling the small rounds of springy dough.

"Now?" Maya was used to paratha on special occasions only. Now she noticed the bowl of cubed potatoes, flecked with spices and fresh coriander.

"No one here to tell me I can't."

She put the water to boil, in a saucepan, Maya noticed with relief. If Shyamma was making masala chai, Maya was not in that much trouble.

"I killed a fish." The words sounded terrible out loud, yet she understood in that moment why criminals confessed. A fleeting lightness lifted in her as she waited for her aunt's absolution.

"Did you eat it?"

"No." What did her aunt think she was? "I tried to save its life."

Shyamma added two teaspoons of tea to the boiling water and some milk. She let it boil vigorously, like the chai wallahs back home did, in huge pots on single burners.

"Sounds like a contradiction."

"It was an accident."

They ate in silence, at the same Formica-topped table Shyamma had bought 20 years ago at a yard sale. The paratha was slightly burnt, crispy at the edges and soft in the middle. Maya couldn't remember when it had tasted so good.

"You don't have to come here every time you want aloo paratha."

Shyamma cleared the dishes as she spoke. Maya had the impression she was going somewhere, that she didn't want her to stay.

"I know." She had the recipe, carefully pasted into a note-book with a number of other recipes Shyamma had insisted on showing her. At the time, she'd resisted; it seemed unnecessary, a leftover from a time when girls prepared for marriage. Perhaps Shyamma had not been preparing her for anyone but herself.

As it turned out, Shyamma did have plans. She was going to a friend's house to discuss their Christmas vacation, a cruise somewhere warm and tropical. Maya hid her surprise; the only holidays her aunt had ever taken were their trips to India. Not wanting to even slightly dissuade her, Maya said nothing. She took the leftover paratha and headed home, with promises to bring Evan back in a few weeks.

When she got home, Evan was out. She went straight to the bedroom and dug around for leftover stars stashed in her bedside table, but there were none. She cleared off the table and stood on it; using the wall for balance, she picked at Orion's belt until she was able to peel away one of the stars. Then she found the wide emptiness she stared at when she couldn't sleep and smoothed the used star into it, directly above her side of the bed. The points curled, the adhesive would not hold. Tomorrow, or the day after or even next week, she would make the bed and her hand would find it, cast out from its home.

All these years, she thought the answer lay in teaching Shyamma to love the cold. Maybe she was wrong.

Maya sat on the porch staring across the river. The sun had nearly set and the air felt like rain, heavy and full of promise. Her skin was clammy from the heat and humidity, but it didn't bother her. It reminded her of the way she felt in the monsoon, just before the rains came, turning the streets into muddy rivers that came up to her knees.

The door opened, and she saw Evan's shadow cast down the stairs. He stood for a moment in the doorway, drinking a beer.

"Nice night," he said.

His voice was low and cautious as he sat down next to her. Maya couldn't bring herself to look at his face, that sweet combination of dimples and blue eyes that showed his confusion no matter how hard he tried to hide it. Instead, she looked at his feet, grimy from a barefoot summer, the toenails ridged and hard, dirt rimming the cuticles. Later, maybe, his nails would scratch dully against her legs, her ankles, and the tops of her feet, leaving white lines and marks across her own dry brown skin, never hard enough to draw blood, but enough to mark Evan on her.

"Shyamma used to have a small shrine in the corner of our kitchen." Her voice was hoarse from thirst and silence. "Incense, flowers, an old calendar painting of Ganesha. That's all. Whenever I had friends over, I'd try to keep them from going in there."

"Why?"

"So I wouldn't have to hear them laugh and say, 'Ew, what's that?' and then explain why my aunt was worshipping a god with an elephant head."

"The god of all beginnings and the remover of obstacles." Evan sat down next to her.

"Shyamma told you that."

"When we got married."

Maya smiled. At the time, she would have forbidden the mention of Ganesha or any other god at her wedding, yet Shyamma had managed to find a space for him.

"I'm going to the temple when she comes."

One day, Shyamma would be gone, and she wanted to be left with more than the calendar image of a pot-bellied elephant god.

Evan took Maya's hand and squeezed it. "Want me to come?"

"It's okay."

Maya drew a sip of beer from the long-necked bottle, letting a few drops drip down her chin. She held the cool glass against her temple and watched the lights come on across the river, solitary stars dotting a dark, lonely land. Evan put his hand on the back of her neck and stroked the damp hairs hanging out of her bun. They sat for a long time in silence, listening to the cicadas buzzing in the still heat, waiting for the storm to break and the sky to clear.

# Small Bang Only

When he left the boatyard in Vladmir's ugly little brown car, with its broken heater and torn seats, Milo headed northwest. In his rearview mirror, he saw the Statue of Liberty fading into the dusk. The day had been unseasonably cold, and now lavender light rimmed the skyline to his west. He turned right on Bourne. In the passenger seat, there was a small suitcase he had found in a thrift store last year when Serafina started her training. He thought she was training to be a secretary, and the suitcase had been a kind of joke, how they had come this far so she could type someone else's letters. Stamped in gold on the worn leather: United Nations. Lake Success, 1950.

Milo drove past a cluster of row houses, cramped and mean with ragged net curtains in the windows and lopsided tricycles on the sidewalk in front. Along Hamilton, he saw the car dealerships and the boarded up windows and scarred doors of the old warehouses, once part of a prosperous industrial neighborhood. It was a landscape he loved and hated, a familiar ruin. Serafina had been less ambivalent. We came to America for a new life, not a reminder of the old one, she said. Last month, a developer bought the entire block and Milo's landlady said the whole place would be razed for condos and retail. Perhaps this development would impress Serafina, she said, her look full of sympathy and pity for her single tenant. Lois was in her sixties, full of energy and life, despite her gray hair and small frame. Milo knew that to her he was pathetic—unshaven, scrawny in baggy jeans and second-hand shirts.

At the corner, Milo passed a brick wall covered in the graffiti of several nations. An international wailing wall. He did not slow down to admire his handiwork of a drunken summer night, the black scrawl of *Serafina is bitch*. He was ashamed now, though the letters were so small and cramped, they were invisible from any distance. He promised himself, as he had for the last three months, that he would go back and insert the article. He would at least be grammatical.

On the ramp to the BQE, traffic moved slowly, and dusk became night. She would be working late all week. It was October, and the big shots were in town. Last year, when she crawled into bed at 1am, exhilarated and exhausted, he had urged her to quit. Perhaps that was the moment when she began to leave him.

By the time he got onto the bridge, all the lights were on, their reflection dancing on the dark water below. He thought he might stop the car, ignore the angry drivers and make his way over to the edge and jump. He had never fully explored this option—it looked so easy in the movies, but reality was complicated by traffic, barriers, and the complex workings of the bridge itself. Besides, the moment for killing himself had passed. It had been an empty threat, uttered in the weeks before she left, and following through with it now would not change the humiliation. Vladmir's solution offered possibilities. You are broken man, he said. You want to feel better. Revenge. I find for you, ultimate revenge. Is a man's job.

The ultimate revenge, Milo thought, might be to sit in traffic like this for a few hours, in an overheated Jetta with a seat that would not adjust and left his knees knocking against the steering wheel. Traffic inched forward; ahead of him, a car had stalled in the left lane and now a red BMW convertible was trying to merge right, in front of a gold Accord. Milo hit the horn; now was not the time for delays. If he waited too long, he would be late. And loose his nerve. That was what Jas had said in the kitchen the other day, "This man is loosing his nerve." And when Milo corrected him, tried to explain the difference between lose and loose, Jas had laughed and said, "You think you're American now, Mr. Serafina?"

Mr. ex-Serafina, sitting in a tin can of a car, that's who he was. Mr. ex-Serafina, without a green card, which he would need now that she and her G-4 visa had left him. Mr. ex-Serafina, who would have to return to a country he left behind if he didn't get "his situation sorted out." That's how Lois, whose son was a lawyer, had put it. Milo watched a smooth cap of platinum blond hair emerge from the passenger's window of the BMW. The hair was perfect, but when she turned her head to face the Honda, Milo lost his breath. The face under the hair was rough, fallen and crushed by age, with thick lips smeared in pink lipstick. Not what he expected, such an old face with such young hair.

The Honda would not give way, and the blonde woman waved at Milo, her face cracked by a hideous smile. He could not let her in; he was late. What did he care if Vladmir's ugly shitbox got scratched? And if the police stopped him, searched the car? Vladmir's car, with Jas's handiwork in the little suitcase in the seat next to him? Maybe they were losers—or loosers—but they were his friends. His only friends, testing him.

Milo honked and let the BMW cut in front of him. The woman smiled and blew a kiss at him. Her teeth, white panels of perfection gleamed, and the deep lines in her face disappeared. Turning back, she yelled something about the time. Or his mind. Milo felt grateful then anxious about his gratitude toward a stranger and her meaningless gesture.

He was on the bridge for a mile, but it took 45 minutes to get to the FDR/Pearl St. ramp heading north. The heat in the car was unbearable, and he rolled down a window, suddenly panicked. Maybe he was too stupid to be nervous, too stupid to worry about the little brown suitcase. Small bang only, Jas had said, as if Milo knew nothing about explosives, as if Milo did not know that a small bang was relative and that when you were picking through the rubble of your office, trying to find the security guard you said good morning to every morning, nothing seemed small, and the sorrow and fear felt infinite. The smell of burning wood and rubber, the chemical taste that lingered for weeks in his mouth, the burning sensation when he blew his nose. After the building he worked in collapsed, his nose bled every night for weeks.

Milo drove slowly, anxious about missing his exit. To his right, the East River shimmered. Had it been three years or four since that Circle Line trip when Serafina pointed to the UN, told him she had heard they needed interpreters? He thought she meant secretaries. He had not known her French was that good, that she would qualify as someone fluent in four languages, and now, so many months later, sick at heart, he was still wondering, what was that fourth language, and had he really been too tired to ask or just stupid?

The garage was around the corner from the exit; he had her old parking pass, valid for another month. Give those fat politicians a shock, Vladmir said. What good they have done for us? With their peace force that takes people to safe area and lets them die? So a few cars are lost, some Swiss, some Dutch. A fair exchange, Vladmir said. He grunted and pulled his pants up over his belly. As far as Milo could tell, Vladmir had always been a short-order cook. But he, like Milo, expected more, giving up one life for another should mean a move up, not down. And had the UN done its job, there would have been no need for this unfair exchange, this giving up of everything you knew and loved for a life of invisibility.

Milo parked the car on the second floor, in the handicapped space near the elevator. He reached for the suitcase next to him. *Lake Success, 1950.* So much for world peace. He thought about the brick wall, covered in error and unhappiness. Had their lives really been so great before? What had they exchanged? Serafina crying as she peeled potatoes. The war had reduced them to this—the men working half days in tenuous conditions, the women cleaning house all day, sobbing over their wasted education. Sometimes Serafina stayed in bed all day, reading one thick English novel after another, the dictionary and a pencil always at hand.

Jas had rigged the bomb so that Milo would not screw it up, would not forget the essential indefinite article that completed the sentence. Milo had taken Jas to the wall the next day and had noticed the error immediately. Shit, he said. Yes, Jas said, reaching under his turban to scratch his head. Now she is not coming back, he said. But Jas did not see the missing article until Milo pointed it out, and later he told Vladmir, and they teased Milo all week, a kind of gentle teasing that only underscored their pity for him. Was this negligible black scrawl the best he could do?

"You the man, my friend," Vladmir said in the boatyard, the smell of sweat and garlic filling the car as he leaned in through the window.

"Yes, I am a man," Milo said, wincing at the misused article, the dropped verb.

Vladmir sighed and shook his head. "The man. You the man. Like on TV."

"This car is junk," Milo said, resisting the urge to continue the discussion of "the" versus "a."

"The world is junk, my friend. The politicians think they can throw away whole country, whole people. Life is cheap."

Lights reflected off the cars behind him, most of them black and sleek. Some had DPL plates, and he wondered why diplomats bothered paying for parking when they could park on the street with impunity. Their children got drunk and ran into lampposts or pedestrians, then quickly disappeared to the home country, covered by immunity. No wonder war criminals got away.

When had Milo become a man without hope? Four years ago, he was a different man when his brother called and said, You're with us or you're with them. Your choice.

If the war had not come, if he had not hung up on his brother mid-sentence—if, if, and if. Nothing was as he expected. When people said New York, they did not think of the shabby neighborhood he had just left behind, its squalid tenements and uneven streets, looking like a war zone itself. He had not expected to work day and night bussing tables, taking shit from illegals while his wife went to school. In this new country, with his halting English, his engineering degree was useless. At home, Serafina had been the housewife. She had been the one washing dishes, holding cracked glasses to the light, scraping leftovers into the garbage. Here, she was the one with the visa.

He just had to open the suitcase, hit the timer, and leave it in the shadow of the trashcan near the elevator.

"Don't think about it," Vladmir said. Too much thinking, no action.

22

There was too much to think about—the tiny kitchen where Serafina wept, the Ministry of Development where he worked, first barricaded, then reduced to frame and rubble. His brother's words. You give up your family for her?

Milo didn't tell Serafina about the phone call. He did not know what had bothered his brother more—her lack of family or her religion. He had never paid attention to his brother's nationalist rants, but after the call Milo felt frightened and worried that he would lose Serafina. War was coming, and it would change everything. They left home in the middle of the night, with two small suitcases and their passports. Milo forced Serafina to leave her books, even though she insisted she'd be able to carry her suitcase. One of the women in their group had brought her small dog, and when she saw it, Serafina cut Milo a look, her blue eyes sharp slivers in a pale round face. They had argued about Aggie, the stray Serafina found a year ago, and when Milo left the cat behind the dumpster in the alley, a month's supply of food piled next to her, Serafina cried and refused to look at him.

She'll be here when we get back, Milo said. You'll see.

There was a long walk, up and down, through quiet suburban streets and wooded areas. Finally, they were at the border. For a moment, Milo thought about letting Serafina go ahead. He remembered he had not seen his mother in a year, not since Serafina's first awkward meeting with her and Novak. His mother's arthritis made it difficult for her to do much around the house, and a fine layer of dust covered the mantle and the framed pictures of Milo and Novak as children, and their father, when he was young, vibrant and alive. His mother had been polite, but Milo could tell she was displeased. Later, on the phone, she said it was not because Serafina was not like us. No, the problem was she was an intellectual, one of those women who would put career before family. Am I to die without grandchildren? Your brother refuses to marry, and you marry this he/she who just wants to be smart.

All that was certain lay behind Milo, and only darkness and uncertainty lay ahead. Twigs snapped underfoot. Someone breathed heavily behind him, wheezing as they slowly walked uphill, their path lit by a couple of weak flashlights. The woman with the dog blew her nose noisily, perhaps weeping for the life she'd left behind. If Milo went home, he'd be okay. He could disappear into these woods and return home during daylight. Serafina would go ahead; she had not looked back since they left the city, and she might not notice his absence until she was safely over the border. He could retrieve the cat and wait for normalcy to return. An engineer would always find work. And in a year or two, or even three if necessary, Serafina would return, they would start their family, the awfulness of their country's disintegration a fading memory.

Before crossing the border, their guide demanded their passports.

These passports won't be worth anything soon, the guide hissed when Milo handed over his and Serafina's passports.

They had the old red ones, one of the most sought after passports when he was a teenager and hitchhiked across Europe. With this red passport, one could travel east, west, everywhere freely, no hassles.

Yours has nearly expired, the guide said. Milo couldn't see his face in the shadow cast by the flashlight, but he heard the disgust in the guide's voice. He didn't understand what difference his passport made; they were entering another country illegally, and if they got caught, having an up-to-date passport would not change anything.

They crossed the border at dawn then hiked through the mountains for two days. They were free. And still, Milo did not tell Serafina about the phone call. In the days and weeks to come, they would read the latest news of destruction and

mayhem, and he would wonder what Novak was doing. Serafina would not know how close he had come to leaving her.

When the elevator opened, Milo had been sitting in the
garage for an hour. A woman with brown hair and a heavy
coat emerged, with a pronounced limp. Milo slouched in his
seat, but she had seen him. She walked over to the car, confi-
dence in every uneven step.

"Is this the second or third floor?" she asked, leaning in
through the open window.

He must have looked confused.

"I'm so tired, I forgot what button I pressed," she said.
"And I don't want to walk to the other side if my car isn't here."

Milo panicked. Was she asking for a ride? He willed
himself not to look at the suitcase. Maybe this was a trick, a
way to get him to give himself up. He felt sweat trickle down
his neck.

"Second floor? Is second floor."

"They'll all be coming down in a few minutes."

"Excuse?"

"Are you waiting for your wife? Girlfriend?"

Milo nodded.

You're always waiting for her, his brother once said, his
voice neutral, the possibility of war still distant.

When she came home after her first week at work, she had
been so happy she could not fall asleep. She stayed up late into
the night, reading, and still seemed rested in the morning.
The arguments started during the first General Assembly
and continued into the following year. "You don't want me to
be happy," she said, a few weeks before she left. She took her
clothes and her books, leaving behind a single white bookcase,
its empty shelves echoing her absence.

The woman limped off towards the other side of the lot.
Why hadn't she parked in the handicapped spot? Maybe

someone else had taken it. Maybe she did not see herself as needing it.

Novak would be Vladmir's age now, early fifties. They had not spoken since that phone call, and for all Milo knew, his brother—older, wiser, once much admired—was dead.

Two women emerged from the elevator, laughing and talking. Their heels rang out on the concrete, and Milo knew before he saw her black hair, that one of them was Serafina. She was wearing black pumps and a skirt that came to her knees. In her arms, she carried a sheaf of papers, and a black briefcase hung over her shoulder. Her gestures were animated, and he felt a pain so sharp in his side, his breath caught and he had to stop himself from crying out.

Milo opened the suitcase. Was this all it took? A broken heart, a sense of injustice, someone to blame?

He could hear voices echoing across the empty garage as he reduced the device to its parts: a badly packed detonator cap, a broken timer, and a small piece of pipe. Vladmir and Jas's idea of a joke. You're with us or you're with them. Not small bang, but no bang. When Milo was done, he snapped the suitcase shut and pushed himself out of the car, his legs stiff and cold, and walked around to where he could be seen. A car approached—a maroon Kia—and slowed down.

"Milo?"

He walked over to the open window. Her face, round and pale, framed by smooth brown hair, was lovelier to him now than ever before. He swallowed hard.

"You left this behind," he said, holding up the case, flashing the gold lettering at her.

Serafina said something to her companion.

"You can put it in the trunk," she said. "It's open."

Milo walked around to the back of the car. The trunk was pristine, unlike Vladmir's with its empty beer cans and old tires. He slammed the lid with a lot more force than he intended and walked back to the window.

"How did you get in?" Serafina asked. Her lipstick was bright red, fresh and glossy. He wanted to ask her where she was going, but it was no longer his business. There was a time when she would have told him, and he wouldn't have listened, or would have only half listened, hearing secretary for interpreter, training for job.

"Remember Aggie?" he said.

"I remember many things."

Voices came from the radio in the car, and the woman in the driver's seat, with her soft jaw line and streaks of gray in her black hair, stared straight ahead.

"There's a little striped cat that sleeps on the back porch of the house. The landlady feeds him. We call him Porch."

He could feel the words tumbling over his tongue. He knew how he looked, in his old canvas coat and jeans, dirty sneakers, shaggy brown hair. Like a refugee.

The driver undid her coat buttons and shifted in her seat until she had pulled her coat off, nearly knocking Serafina in the face.

"Miloje," Serafina said. Her eyes were clear and steady behind her glasses. When had she started wearing glasses full time?

"He left us for a while. She said he was sowing his oats. I thought he was dead."

"What do you want?"

He wanted to know why she was speaking English. He wanted to know why she never asked about his brother, his mother, his younger sister. Didn't she want to know why he never called home? But this woman with Serafina's face was a stranger, as strange to him as the brother who threatened him. He thought of the weeks she spent calling the neighbors to find out if Aggie was okay, and how he had ignored her crying.

He could have been a better husband; she could have been a better wife.

"I want to go home," Milo said and returned to the car.

After a moment, he heard the KIA drive away. He started the Jetta. A blast of cold air hit him. In minutes, the car would be hot again. How to explain it all to Vladmir and Jas? He didn't think he could find the words in English. In the rear view mirror, Milo saw a flash of red, the fender of a car parked in the corner. He remembered the gold Honda, the BMW. The smile of a total stranger. Her kiss. Her words, in slow motion.

*You are so kind.*

# I Brake for Moose

**Friendly's 1:30 am**

We are sitting at a booth, brown vinyl with scratches and holes burned into it from too many careless cigarettes over the years, shooting M&M's back and forth across the table. A cigarette burns close to the butt, still I take a drag, too tired to care that I'm into my second pack of the day. I will quit when we get back to New York. I will quit the next time I hear the band's single on the radio. I will quit the day Gus and Jeremy show up anywhere on time. All remote possibilities, too distant to measure anything by.

"I read this article about these Indian guys who dump their American girlfriends to marry wives their parents pick for them," Joanne says. She looks like a ferret, dark eyes ringed hollow with thick eye liner that never seems to smear, no matter how hard she dances, how late we stay up. Her face is small and pointy, her brown hair cut in layers, short and crooked, close to her scalp. Her skin is sallow, washed out like salted cod soaked for too many days.

I've been reading about the depletion of cod in the Grand Banks, the migrations of the fishing industry up and down the coast. I've been reading about the Acadian Forest, where descendants of Frenchmen fleeing the British in Canada still speak French. I've been reading about Baxter State Park, where moose and other wildlife roam freely. I'm reading about the landscape we never see because we're still sleeping it off by the time tomorrow rolls around. Joanne's reading her horoscope in a magazine, which is where she comes across the article.

"Some of them even get married, on a trip to the old country, and then come back and pick up with their girlfriends as if nothing's changed."

I yawn and push a green M&M towards her; it rolls off the table but she doesn't notice.

"I've only met Gus's parents twice," she says. "You know, in the whole time we've been together, I've only met them. Never eaten with them, had a drink, nothing. Do you think that's weird?"

I know girls who live with their boyfriends and have two separate phone lines. I know girls who outright lie, tell their parents he's the roommate's brother, a nice guy from a good family. But we're talking about Joanne, Joanne and Gus, the Romeo and Juliet of the road. I don't really have to answer her, I've learned, just look sympathetic, scowl in the appropriate places, and eat her leftover fries.

"More coffee?"

It's Alma, our waitress, blond hair, cut short to her head, almost like Joanne's, closer to a cap than a bad wig. She's young, too young for such an old name, and her lipstick is soft glossy pink. I feel sorry for her, so I nod even though my stomach is burning; the inside probably looks like the bench we're sitting on right now.

Waiting is what we do best, all for the privilege of being able to say, "I'm with the band," and walk past the red velvet ropes and other girls as if we've done something special. This has happened only twice in the six months I've been around, once in Boston, where there are a lot of college students and women's colleges, so it doesn't really count, and once in New York, when we opened for another, better known band. "We" is what Joanne, official girlfriend of the lead singer, says. We are with the band, she says, and the way she says it, rhythmically, with resonance, it's like a mantra she must tell herself when I'm not listening.

### How I Got Here

My parents want to know what kind of an Indian name is Gus.

"I don't know."

A boy from a good family, last name known to my parents, caste equal to ours, theirs not mine since I don't understand any of that stuff—that is Gus, and I should feign more interest in him as he is the reason I am "allowed" to go on the road with the band. Officially, I tell my parents, I am the treasurer since I have a head for numbers.

"One last fling," I promise, as I did four years ago when I dropped out of grad school in Pittsburgh and fled to New York.

"But they can't say anything," Joanne says. She listens to my phone calls then tries to tell me how I should talk to my parents. "You've been supporting yourself since you graduated."

"It doesn't work like that."

She says, "Oh?"

And then I have to explain, explain that immigrant children are expected to succeed and capture all the remaining bits of the American dream that eluded their parents. They are not expected to drop out of business school, work a series of clerical jobs, send home a new address and phone number every six months, promising that this time the apartment will work out. It's not like Joanne can't understand. Her father tells her he didn't slave in a mill for thirty years, just outside of Worcester, so she could go to Smith and become a friggin' secretary, working the night shift at a production company that does special effects for TV commercials that he mutes anyway: Huggies, Nationwide Insurance, the US Marines.

We were bored, Manhattan was hot, and the band had a single that was, unbelievably, getting some airplay. It was time, Gus said, to hit the college circuit, build up a following. We were heading north and would be back before Christmas.

This is what I tell my parents, promise to call them collect. I tell them Gus is a nice guy, the brother I never had. I tell them the band is on the verge of success, almost famous. I tell them the boys all went to college, Ivy League schools up and down the East Coast.

### What I Don't Tell My Parents
Kenny, the drummer, is twenty-nine, maybe older, definitely older than the rest of us, six credits short of a degree in something he can no longer remember. We think it's the dope, killed too many brain cells, but good drummers are hard to find.

On and off stage, Gus has the moves of someone who thinks he's a star. He has a mop of black curly hair, a long, thick nose, high cheekbones and brown eyes like pools. That's how Joanne describes them, pools of dark light she'd like to drown in. I think she got that from one of her magazines. On the road, people assume Gus and I are brother and sister even though we look nothing alike: my skin is lighter, my nose flatter, and my face rounder. My hair is straight and long, and the closest we get to being brother and sister is that we both sound the same, products of private schools and New England colleges.

When we first met, we realized quickly that our parents move in the same circles but have never met and this knowledge becomes a sheer curtain between us before I've even decided whether I like him or not. We got into a fight about the money some towns back and didn't talk at all for a few days, but Gus knows I'm right—band expenses are not the same as personal bar tabs—so he's not openly hostile. We've sized each other up several times now and keep a wary distance like dogs on alert.

The rules are simple: the band comes first and personal conflicts must be contained at any cost.

I should tell my parents about Mike, the guitarist, who is from Minnesota and knows the Laura Ingalls Wilder house well. He is short and stands a bit like a duck, all swayback and butt, but it's not something you'd notice when he's on stage. He wears plaid and thermal and big thick hiking boots. His girlfriend, Christine, works on Wall Street and thinks Joanne and I are losers.

Did I mention that we all went to Smith? Women's college, serious degrees: Economics, History, Math? Did I mention that Christine has a job on Wall Street?

Finally, I don't tell my parents the real reason I am here, sitting in a Friendly's with winter breathing down my back. I don't tell them about Jeremy, the long summer nights we spent drinking Bohemia and watching the sun set over the Hudson from the sixth floor walk up Joanne and I shared, and the short autumn nights now, when we turn our backs to each other and fall into troubled, unrestful sleep. I don't tell them about those days when I used to stand in front of the stage and watch the top of his blond head, bent over that bass like he was studying for an exam, and how I stood and waited for the small flicker of recognition, the smile, the wink, the nod that would come when he finally looked up and saw me. Perpetually tan, long and thin, he was sunshine in those dank basement bars, a rock steady beat in the chaotic boredom of my carefree life.

And now I felt the chill of unrelieved togetherness, too soon after our summer romance, like a layer of snow over the first spring daffodils. Everything that had been good and fun between us lay in the past like permafrost, impenetrable, static, and cold to the touch.

### Friendly's 2:00 am

We're still waiting, cigarette butts spilling over, coffee grown cold at the bottom of white cups stained with lipstick and bits of tobacco. I eat some of Joanne's French fries, feel sick to my stomach. Mike dropped us off at one, then took the car back to help finish packing up. With girls milling around, breaking down the equipment always took longer than it should. I got the money, cash that I stowed in a cloth purse around my neck, in between my t-shirt and my wool sweater. I divide the money five ways: Mike, Kenny, Gus, Jeremy, and the band. A percentage always goes to band costs, which includes my salary, a sum so low, I probably won't have to file income taxes this year.

Alma stands at her station, smoking a cigarette. Another waitress who has just come in says something to her. Alma looks over at the door and shakes her head. She stopped asking if we wanted more coffee some time ago.

"We should pay," I say. "Let her go home." There's something familiar about her, but I can't place her face.

Joanne shrugs. She has an amazing capacity for long hours of doing nothing. She doesn't overeat, drink, or even chip her nail polish. She was a history major, someone who memorized scores of dates and facts and stories about things everyone else has forgotten, and now she sits here without a thought in her head.

"Do you think Gus will leave me for an Indian girl? Some nice virgin his parents find?"

So this is where we are.

### What Else I Don't Tell My Parents

When I called my parents yesterday, I told them everything was fine, the foliage was beautiful, and the sun was shining on the water, a perfect blue sky day. I told them the band was playing well, that we would soon be in Canada, New Brunswick to be precise, then Nova Scotia where Gus had friends, and after that we'd turn around and start our way back home. We had played harvest parties, fall frolics and frat formals, half empty bars and wedding receptions, arranged by every connection we could pull. On the way back, a couple of Christmas parties and then we'd be home. I said it like that, we'd be home, as if I too were now part of the band.

I don't tell them I have to drive for Kenny because he has no sense of direction, and the last time we let him drive the van, he passed three exits before he realized he should have gotten off the highway 30 miles ago. I don't tell them about the marijuana seeds on the floor of the van. I don't tell them I'm tired, that my back hurts and my stomach feels hollow most days.

And I won't tell them about the day before, about how we got three rooms at the HoJo's when we arrived at dawn because we hadn't gone to sleep yet, and how Jeremy stayed in Gus and Joanne's room, to work out the play list while I crawled into bed in the same smoky t-shirt I'd been wearing for the last 24 hours and popped two Benadryls and still couldn't sleep.

A couple of hours later, as light begins to seep in through the sides of the curtain that doesn't quite cover the window, Jeremy sags into bed, his clothes still on. We say nothing, which is mostly what we do these days when we're alone, exhausted, wrung out, this has not been as much fun as I thought it would be, and Jeremy feels the weight of that. It's not his fault, I want to tell him, but in that musty, overheated room with its worn blue carpet and ashtray full of someone else's butts, there is no space to say what I really feel.

After a while, he says, "What are you thinking?"

I'm thinking about cold baths in the claw foot tub in the kitchen with the old black and white TV on the dining table and a bottle of wine on the little plank that rests across the top of the tub. He'd come in, after practice or a double shift at the diner, and I'd run the bath, it was that hot and humid still. Joanne was working late or at Gus's, and in the glow of the TV, I'd lean into Jeremy, shiver, and watch our shadowy limbs in the cold water, long fish in a dark aquarium. Afterwards, we'd pad along the floor to my narrow bedroom without the door and make love in near darkness because the room faced the alley behind the building and got almost no light. When Jeremy was there, I didn't hear the clang of the garbage cans being opened, the sound of bottles shattering on concrete, the howling of stray cats in heat. I remember every hair and sinew and vein on his arms, the arms that cradled that bass, and I felt no jealousy, only envy at the sureness with which Jeremy played. He would be a bass player his entire life; a degree from Yale wouldn't change that, he said, and to prove it, he took the crappiest jobs he could find so all his energy could go into his music.

He always left after a few hours. I didn't mind because I slept better alone. My room was narrow and cramped, a mattress on the floor of a closet and even though Joanne said we could use her bed, a double futon in a room at the front of the apartment, for both the act of Jeremy leaving and the fact of me sleeping alone troubled her, we did not. By some unspoken agreement, we understood that neither of us could imagine making love in someone else's bed.

The bed in our room is soft and wide, with enough space for both of us to sleep comfortably. We try, curl up against each other, then shift and return to the edges, as far away from the dip in the middle, the one I hadn't noticed when I lay down alone. After a few hours, Jeremy gets up to take a shower and when he comes out, he finds me staring at the ceiling.

"What are you thinking?" he asks again. His green eyes are miserable, but I can't look at him for I don't want him to see mine. Not dark pools of light but murky bog land from which nothing emerges.

We cannot, of course, break up on the road, disturb the tender ecosystem we have struggled to maintain for the last two months. But we can find a space apart. So, in the after-noon, when Joanne says she wants to hang out at the hotel until the party starts, Jeremy agrees and I take off with Kenny and Gus. Mike, it goes without saying, will stay behind, make sure everything's good to go. We plan to meet again at seven, then head over to the student union to set up.

We end up at a bar, which is where you always end up with Kenny and Gus, off the side of a single lane road that grows progressively darker as the sun sets behind the trees that loom sky-high on either side of it. The bar is in a clearing, near a pizza parlor and Chinese restaurant with bright neon lights. The parking lot is crowded, the bar filled with slightly too old high school students dressed for the prom, young men with pimply faces and shag haircuts in ill-fitting pastel colored tuxedos and women, girls younger than me really, in matching dresses shaped and cut like elaborate lampshades.

Gus is buying, and before I can decide if I want to stay, there's a cold beer in my hand, and Kenny has disappeared. The small room with wood-paneled walls, low rough beams and a high shiny bar is packed with dazed, mildly drunk people. I feel conspicuous, me and Gus dark blips on a white landscape.

"Don't worry," Gus says, wielding a roll of quarters. "The bartender said we could hang. It's his cousin's wedding."

Into the jukebox, five dollars worth of quarters, all oldies, the songs the band used to cover when they first started in college, years before my time. We feed the jukebox, line up the songs Kenny's cousin Louise asked for at her wedding last summer. Mike, Jeremy, and Gus argued over the right mix of originals and covers, and the ever-changing play list reflects the continuing discussion. Standing in front of the jukebox, now, Gus and I exclaim over our favorites, forget the arguments, the money, the mutual suspicion that has dogged us since the day we met. The Stones, Janis Joplin, Marvin Gaye, Aretha. Led Zeppelin and T-Rex, for the sake of high school.

"Only girls listen to T-Rex," Gus sneers, as I hit the button.

Gus dances. He dances with me, passes me off to Kenny, dances with the bride, the groom, and his best man, and a blond girl, more than once. She is lithe and small, petite like Joanne so that she doesn't quite reach Gus's shoulder. I watch them from the bar, talk to Kenny, turn around to get another beer, and when I look into the center of the room, they're gone. It's only six, and I'm not worried, just glad to be away, away from Joanne and her endless inquiry into a future I cannot see and my broken relationship with Jeremy. Then T-Rex is on and Gus pulls me out onto the dance floor. When the song turns into a slow one, I feel his warm palm on my back, my cold hand in his.

"Are you cold?"

I shake my head, and he folds my fingers into his. He is only a couple of inches taller than me, but I cannot look at his lips, full and soft, surrounded by a rough five o'clock shadow so I focus instead on the patch of skin between his neck and his chest. And then the song is over, and in the distance I hear a bottle crash against the wall. The wedding party is drunk. Night has fallen, and I know if we stay another minute, I won't be able to get us back to where we came from. So I take Gus's hand and pull him through the mass of people packed around us. Near the door, he drains his beer, and Alma—whose name I didn't know, who I wouldn't recognize hours later at Friendly's—gossamer winged angel in pink netting and taffeta, steps out of a group at the bar and hands Gus a folded piece of paper.

"Later?" she says, ignoring me.

He puts the paper in his shirt pocket and pats it reassuringly, reaches over to touch her cheek.

Outside, Gus says, "She thinks you're my sister." We are still holding hands. The air is a cold shock, but it's the sky, the perfect star-studded sky edged with the ragged tops of pine, spruce and fir, it's this sky that stops us in our tracks, takes my breath away, and makes Gus squeeze my hand.

"Jeremy," I start to say.

"I know," Gus says, and squeezes my hand one more time. I open my mouth to speak, but nothing comes, only a flood of tears that soak his shoulder. I see Jeremy, frozen in a photograph wearing the shirt I bought him before we hit the road, and I wonder if sadness will always look like a light blue shirt with small paisleys in red and green. Finally, I look up and Gus kisses me, gently but not in a brotherly way, not in a way I could later justify to my parents, Jeremy, myself or Joanne. I step back and wipe my lips.

"That was a stupid thing to do," I say. I blow my nose and walk away.

Perhaps Joanne is right, the only way to get to the border is to turn your eyes back to your magazine, look away from the intensity of these boys who know exactly what they want to do.

"You think too much," Gus says, as we get into the smoke-filled van.

"Or maybe not enough," Kenny says, from the back seat. He's been waiting for us and hands me the roach between his fingers.

I stub it out in the ashtray.

"Ken, tell me you didn't smoke that whole thing by yourself," Gus says, worried now about the gig. The girl at the bar, the kiss at the door, we've been filed and forgotten.

I pull out of the parking lot, the taste of beer and smoke on my lips, along with something foreign I cannot name. When we get home, Jeremy keeps saying, as if somehow that will erase the nights of sleeping in our clothes, on beds that sag in the middle but still do not bring us closer together. When we get home, I'll still be smoking. When we get home, I'll still be looking. When we get home, Jeremy says, everything will be better, you'll see this will all be worth it.

All I thought I'd wanted was for one brief moment to be able to say, "I'm with the band." Now I'm coming up empty, and as the van hurtles down the winding road, brights cutting the path through the darkness, I want to blame someone for my insides-hollowed-out, but when I look around, there's no one, just myself.

### Friendly's 2:30 am

We're waiting, and by now I've realized that Alma is the girl from the bar and she's waiting too. I wonder if Joanne and I should leave, then remember that we have no car or van. Besides, Joanne won't have it. Her job is to wait: she waits for the set to start, then she's the first one on the floor, close to the stage where she can smile at Gus when he looks at her. Then, after the show, she waits—she doesn't help load out, she just waits, watches the action through the smoke generated by endless packs of cigarettes and the constant crunch of peanut M&M's.

"Do you think Gus would want a traditional Indian wedding?" she asks. "What are they like?"

"Lots of standing around and waiting for something to happen," I say. "I went to sleep during my uncle's."

"It could be fun," she says, looking at her watch then the door as a heavy man in a fur cap sweeps in.

Our job is to wait. Waiting is what we do best.

### How We Get There

Tonight, somewhere in Maine, the harvest moon hangs low in the sky and for a brief moment I imagine the world is coming to an end, a moon that big and orange surely has Wellsian implications. I feel relief at the thought of this; with the world at an end, so ends the tour. No more hours upon hours of trying to get Kenny to give me the wheel as he takes yet another wrong turn. No more M&M and French-fry dinners. No more smiling when I really feel like screaming.

After the bar, Kenny and I dropped Gus off at the hotel for a quick shower and picked up Mike.

"See you in ten," Gus said.

Mike looked at his watch and muttered, "Ten years or ten hours?"

The harvest moon disappears behind the trees and shrubs on the side of the road, emerges a few miles later, still glowing like a pearly orange. We arrive at the plain brick building, an oddly quiet and unpopulated student union, and drive around to the back, where it supposedly will be easier to unload the van. Mike taps the back of the seat with his fingertips, going over music only he can hear. Part of his ritual prep for each gig involves listening to no other music for the hours preceding it, which means when I drive him and Kenny, I'm pretty much listening to the voices in my head. The collar to Mike's white thermal shirt, visible at the neck of LL Bean's best scotch plaid, is fraying. Christine would not approve, but perhaps this explains Mike's attraction to the road.

We wait for fifteen, twenty minutes, wait in the increasingly cold van for the mud-splattered station wagon Gus's dad gave him to pull in beside us.

Kenny fires up the roach in the ashtray.

"Jeez, Ken," I say. "Can't you wait just a couple of hours?"

Mike reaches forward, plucks the roach from Kenny's hand, and stamps it out on the van floor.

"Careful," Kenny says, but Mike ignores him. He's the only one who dares, the only one who seems to forget how long it takes to find a new drummer, one who can be relied on to show up and keep tempo. Kenny's the closest we've come, but that isn't saying much. The trick, we've discovered, is to leave the stomped out roaches on the van floor where he can retrieve them later.

The purse hanging from my neck settles against my chest, as if it contains gold coins rather than a handful of twenties, all that's left until we get paid tonight. I blow my bangs out of my face, curse Gus and Jeremy for being late, and pull open the doors to the van and jump back. A guitar stand crashes to my feet.

"Watch out," Kenny says, reaching past me for the pads. He's still mad at me about the dope, even though it's Mike who took it away.

The steel door of the building screeches open, and there's a kid, pimples and long stringy hair, waving us in. He wears worn topsiders without socks and a thick blue sweater.

"Need some help?" he asks. Puffs of smoke fill the air between us, and I grunt and hand him Jeremy's bass.

I'm the girlfriend, I tell myself. I'm with the band, not in the band. I should be sitting in some VIP lounge sipping cocktails, smoking imported cigarettes. I should be wearing a black and blue tie-dyed mini-skirt with thick black tights and blue jellies, not jeans and scuffed Doc Martens, sticky with beer and spiked fruit punch.

I search the van and find and hold the roach not damaged by Mike, and then I run into a stand of evergreens to the right of the parking lot. Through the dark branches, I can see the sky, spotted with stars, white flecks of paint against an illuminated blackboard. The air is crisp and smells of burnt wood, apples and pumpkin pie. If only I could stay here, disappear into the trees, merge with them like moose so that no one would ever find me.

And then I hear tires on gravel, a door opening, and voices that crack the silence like brick through glass. The world is not coming to an end, I am not a moose, and the boys have arrived.

### The Best Years of Our Lives

The boys play a song, a Beatles cover. Gus engages in unnecessary stage banter. They play their hit single, then the B-side. Three people dance, including Joanne. I stand at the back of the auditorium, crush my cigarettes in a red plastic ashtray that Will, the guy who let us in, found for me.

He says, "It's still early. More people will be here soon."

He says, "These guys are wicked good. Glad we could get them."

He says, "You and the lead singer—you guys related or something?"

"Or something," I say, and drink the tepid beer in my hand.

The room is dark and kids lurk in the shadows, with plastic cups of beer and red wine, purchased from a wooden counter in the back corner. Track lights illuminate the raised platform where the band plays at the front of the room, under a big painted harvest moon, complete with craters and pockmarks. Orange and brown streamers hang from the molding.

Jeremy tunes his bass with the mike on. Kenny blows big pink bubblegum bubbles in between songs. He winks at someone I can't see. Gus and Jeremy talk; the play list, peppered with more originals than covers, has once again been abandoned. They play two more songs, Rolling Stones and The Who. Mike says something about moose, Minnesota and Maine, but now there are thirty people on the dance floor, twenty-nine for whom each song sounds new and fresh, not like something they've heard on the radio a thousand times before. Some of the girls wear wrap-around skirts over long johns, heavy boots that make the floor bounce every time they do the pony. The boys jerk stiffly or else flail their arms wildly, making no pretence to stay in time. They are pale from days and nights in a place where winter comes early, and summer comes late. They are in the middle of the best years of their lives, only none of them will know this until that time has passed, and one morning, you wake up in a room the size of your college dorm closet, kill another cockroach in your bathtub, and open an empty refrigerator, not because pay day is two weeks away, but because the depression that sits on you like an oppressive New York summer day has not lifted and it's now the middle of winter, and you're still saying, it will be okay when summer comes. And summer comes and goes, and your fridge is briefly filled by love and a new boyfriend, but even this is not enough, so you take a trip, thinking if you can leave it all behind somehow you'll find what you're looking for.

And what you realize is this: loneliness feels the same no matter where you are, and the ecosystem you're now part of is so delicate a sneeze could blow it apart. Kisses under a star-strewn sky mean nothing, friendships are for the moment, and one stop after another—marked not by lobster nets, or moose or the birch and spruce and pine that tower over the road but by the orange and blue HoJo's and the red and yellow striped cheeriness of Friendly's—one stop becomes the next and pretty soon all the songs on the play list sound the same.

**Friendly's 3:00 am**

Two plates of fries, one cheeseburger (for me) and a million cups of coffee later, the guys show up. Jeremy slides in next to me, Gus next to Joanne, then he says, "Hey, let me sit next to my sister." They switch, Joanne laughs, a deep, husky laugh, and I feel Gus's thigh pressed against mine and try not to shift. Looking at him next to me, I see that Alma's now in Jeremy's line of vision, off to my right, hidden from Gus by my head and the partition between the booths. I wonder what he'll do when she comes to our table.

What he does is what he always does: he and Jeremy order grilled cheese and bacon sandwiches, extra well-done fries, and two Cokes. He smiles at Alma, puts his arm over the back of the booth, rests his fingers lightly on my shoulder.

She bites her lower lip, holds her pen in a childlike way, tight between her fingers and her thumb, pressing down on the pad in her hand. Looking at her, I feel like crying. What did Gus say to her on the dance floor as he held her close and stroked her cheek? What promises did he whisper in her ear that made her hand him that piece of paper, the one he scribbled on between sets when they changed the play list? And who is she that she can imagine a future in his words?

All night I've been looking for the words to tell Joanne that if Gus leaves her, it will not be for a mysterious virgin, fresh off the plane from Delhi. She knows as well as I do that the day she stops showing up at the front of the stage, the day she starts standing at the back of the room, smoking and drinking as if she's heard these songs a million times before, the day she emerges from her world of magazines and remembers she graduated from college with honors, that's the day he'll leave her, and it won't be for some girl like me or a better version, hand-picked by his parents. It will be for Alma, the young girl who imagines that all things are possible if you attach yourself to the fender of a car that's going somewhere. She doesn't see the way night closes in on us early these days, a blink and the sun is gone and the trees press down on us as the car rounds the corner of that dark single lane highway that cuts through a forest of secrets we already know.

When Gus leaves, he will leave for Alma who still imagines a future open with promise and opportunity like a brand new calendar on New Year's Eve.

### How I Leave

I get on a bus. At six in the morning, the depot is closed, the air is cold, but there are people waiting for the first bus to Portland, so I know I've come to the right place. In the reflection of a window, I see dark circles under my eyes, dry chapped lips, and the hollow look of a girl who once was with the band.

I left a note propped against the ashtray, no excuses or explanation, only a good-bye and the band's money. As I shut the door, I imagined Jeremy turning over, reaching for my side of the bed in his sleep, sighing with satisfaction. But as I lean against the brick wall of the depot, sip vending machine coffee that burns my fingers through the paper cup, it's the boy with the wild black hair I'm thinking of, the wide hand on the small of my back, the black hair in the V of his shirt, its whiteness crisp like snow against the darkness of his skin. I feel his hand in mine, as I pull him through a pack of people, and when I turn back to look, he's gone: the hand is someone else's, the face I can't see on a body I don't know.

From my window seat on the bus, I watch daylight creep in. We speed by thickets on either side of the highway, and in a clearing, where I least expect it, a young moose, small and vulnerable, stands and watches us go by. It happens so quickly,

I'm sure I imagined it, but the woman in front of me shrieks, "Moose!" to her young son and taps the window.

I think about what I'll tell my parents, and what I'll tell them is this: I saw some moose, some stars, and some trees. I'll tell them I got tired of waiting. I'll tell them that for one brief moment I could say "I'm with the band," and that perhaps that's all I needed: a moment so brief that years from now, when they tell me Gus is getting married, I'll nod as if I still remember him and go back to whatever it is I'm doing.

# Missing Men

When Meriam returned to work the day after the bomb unit descended on the building, it was still there, the old converted warehouse by the river, strands of yellow police tape snapping in the wind like obscene party streamers. Other than the tape, there were no signs of the previous day's activities, not in the lobby, not in the elevator. And when she opened the office door, she felt the tight knot in her stomach ease slightly. Nothing had been disturbed, nothing moved. The lights were off, the blinds drawn. At first glance, everything was as she had left it.

The office seemed frozen, in that moment between yesterday and today, and now she waited for Clyde to show up with a color corrected cover. He could be elusive in his artist's search for perfection. With him, there was always another idea, a better line, a cleaner look. Meriam was making decisions that the boss usually made, covering for his absence, trying to keep things moving as smoothly as possible. She had been trying to rope Clyde in, corral him, force him to hand over a cover. She called him every day last week, left messages or hung up when he did not answer. She offered to meet him for dinner, her treat, and even suggested she take the train out to his place, pick the cover up herself. She knew he would not go for that, and if anything, the idea of her showing up at his apartment might be enough to jolt him into action.

This morning, she thought she'd seen him in the subway, walking away from the exit as she walked towards it. Out of the corner of her eye, in a throng of people, she saw a tall black man in a raincoat, his head bent over a cell phone, walking against the crowd, brushing against the tiled wall of the platform. She tried to turn around, reach for him, but the tidal pressure of people at her heels was too much. When she was finally able to look back at the emptying platform, he was gone. In less than a minute he had disappeared.

Meriam scanned the room for signs of a search and seize, for misplaced files, for boxes torn open and pillaged. In the corner, by the door, the neat stack of boxes containing the galleys stood intact, unmolested. Accusatory, blaming her for not moving more quickly, saying in their stolid brownness the things Kemal would not. He was not only the book's author but also the boss's lawyer now, called in last month when Vijay was first arrested. When Kemal had phoned her the morning after Vijay's arrest, she thought it was about the book; instead, he told her about the men who had come during the night and taken Vijay away. She was not to let anyone take anything from the office, but by then it was too late, they had come and gone, taking Vijay's computer, his old-fashioned rolodex, his desk calendar with the big squares filled in with deadlines and appointments.

Three men had sifted through files, pored over the bulletin board, looked through her calendar, asked dumb questions, mispronounced names, seized things with a randomness that suggested they did not know what they were looking for.

They took the computer, leaving behind coffee stains, the smell of sesame oil and oyster sauce, and an office awash with paper, everywhere she looked, piles and piles of paper, spilling out from disarranged files. They took three cardboard boxes, including one filled with newspaper and magazine clippings the boss had collected over the years, clippings from *Life*, *Time*, and *India Illustrated Weekly*, sent to him by his cousins in Bombay.

And that was how Kemal's book about the proposed wall between Mexico and Texas had been delayed. They only did two books a year; the books, Vijay said, allowed for politics in a way the newspaper, serving both the community and advertisers, could not. The border book was the press's most controversial book to date, containing information from government documents leaked to Kemal. The bound galleys were almost ready to go when Vijay was arrested.

This time, the men took nothing. Meriam didn't know if they had found a bomb in the building or if it was another abandoned lunch bag. Her coffee from the day before was still in its place on her desk. Her pencil lay across the yellow legal pad, exactly where she'd left it. The telephone blinked with a message from Clyde, promising to show up for dinner. "Let's meet early. It's supposed to snow, and you know I'm not leaving my house once that starts."

Clyde was finicky about weather. At least he had agreed to meet. Meriam opened the cabinet where Vijay kept employee files. She could write a check for Clyde on the spot, keep him from coming in to the office. The less he—and the other freelancers—saw, the longer she could keep Vijay's secret. Even if Kemal had not told her to keep his arrest to herself, she would have done so automatically, more out of habit than loyalty. Variously, she told clients and freelancers that Vijay was on vacation, sick or out of the office. If they didn't ask, she didn't say. She left a fresh half-filled mug of tea on his desk every day, moved his papers around, restacked his books, sharpened and blunted his pencils. She put the proofs of the bi-weekly immigrant newspaper they produced on his desk, as if waiting for his approval. The next day, she moved them to hers. Sometimes she balled up his worn brown cardigan and shoved it into his bottom drawer; a few days later, she would drape it casually over the back of his chair, letting one arm droop to the floor, imitating Vijay's lack of concern for anything other than work.

They had paid Clyde last month. When she rearranged the files after Vijay's arrest, she had seen Clyde's file. Or at least she had not noticed its absence. Now it was gone.

Panic was useless. Meriam knew that jumping to conclusions meant landing in emptiness, in that chasm between fact and fiction that left you flailing for something to hold on to. She was more cautious than that. She knew that if she stopped looking, she would find him: Clyde who hated snow.

The first time she saw snow? a co-worker asked, once he realized she was African. But she couldn't remember the first time—she'd always known snow, it seemed. There had been skiing lessons since before she could remember, on the slopes of Zermatt, Gstaad, Klosters, other snow-capped peaks that formed the landscape of her childhood.

"I can't remember," she had said, and Guy (whose name she could not forget) had walked away in disbelief, convinced she was telling him it snowed in Africa—which it did, only he never asked where. He did not ask her where she was from, but she would not have told him. She was not interested in hearing him say blandly, "Oh, yeah. Where all those people were starving." The distinction was meaningless. On these shores, her people were African, indistinguishable from all the other Africans lining up to get in.

As if she had ever stood on line, anywhere. A lifetime of private tutors, embassy parties, first-class travel all over the world had left her unprepared for the ignorance of the average American, an ignorance that both served her well and irritated her enormously. England had been easier, but after high school, she wanted the freedom of America. And, at the well-known women's college her guardian insisted she and her sister attend, she found a provincialism that shocked her into a watchful silence that others interpreted as arrogance.

She'd had a student visa, then stayed, got one job after another at various multinational banks that valued her private school accent, her languages (French, German, Italian, English). No African languages? Not even Swahili? The interviewers tried to hide their surprise. She didn't explain that because of who she was, she had all the languages she needed.

Work was easy. Wherever she went, work was her home. In an anonymous Sheraton in Copenhagen, with its uniform rooms and sanitary conformity, she would find home the moment she set up her laptop and got on the phone. She made deals, had nice lunches and dinners, traveled, banked bonuses that would have made her brother cry (with envy or frustration, she didn't know, only knew that he would cry because she had something he didn't, even if it was something he didn't want).

Three years ago, they began firing people. Downsizing, they said. An economy weakened by an endless war, they did not say. Less international business, they said, instead.

She had brought in over $10 million in deals, trade agreements in two continents, three languages. She thought she was safe. Then Guy, who after several years had worked his way onto her team, said, as if seeing her for the first time, "You look familiar." And then, a few days later, "You look like that ex-finance minister," and he snapped his fingers, as if trying to recall the scandal he'd read about some years ago. This was not a benign get-to-know-you. His narrow eyes, caught in the folds of his super-sized cheeks, gleamed. She saw that she had overestimated his ignorance, or rather, underestimated his ambition. "Aren't you from—" and she had cut him off. "London," she said, and marched back to her office, her head thumping, her ears ringing and hot.

She could not afford the suggestion of imperfection, she with her green card and foreign languages. Whatever he had figured out, it would be enough to taint her, make her a potential liability. She was descended from a lineage that history did not remember kindly. Or fully, for that matter. Only the abuses, the rumored Swiss bank accounts, the terror and squalor of dictatorship.

She would not wait for the supervisor's hollow excuses, echoing bland magazine headlines she might have read at a newsstand while waiting for change. Meriam would not let them fire her. She would avoid Guy, with his crisp white shirts, his hale and hearty façade, his inquiry into her past. He would look up one day, and she would be gone, and with her, all the answers to his questions.

On her last day, Meriam waited until after seven, then reduced the sum of ten years to a box: ink cartridges for her Waterman pen, an extra pair of sunglasses, two packs of hose, a pair of black suede court shoes, her planner, a crystal paperweight, a calendar with desert landscapes, and an ashtray from the Sheraton in Copenhagen. It had been a gift, given to her long before she went to Copenhagen, long before she stayed at the Sheraton.

She left the drawers to her desk open. She slid her letter of resignation under her supervisor's door. She walked out of the building without looking back, threw the ugly paperweight, her ten-year anniversary gift from the office, into the nearest dumpster.

She had lost so much more.

She was tired of explaining herself. Whenever someone looked too closely at her, she expected the inevitable, the where are you from and how long have you been here. Nowadays, the "when are you going back?" hung as the third, unasked question.

Although 6 o'clock was too early for dinner, Meriam knew it was pointless to argue with Clyde, assuming she could even reach him on the phone. On her way to meet him, she ran into Mr. Lao, who worked down the hall. He stood by the elevator, as if he had been waiting for her. He was from Singapore and ran an import-export business. What exactly he imported or exported was unclear. Meriam thought she might ask him one day, but she did not want to invite nosey questions from him in return. Today, however, was not that day. Before she could say hello, Mr. Lao launched into his latest grievance. A badly made pipe bomb had been found in his office, he announced, complaining about the way they had turned his office inside out, left it in such a mess, it would take weeks for him to recover the project he was working on. He told Meriam they came (he did not specify who) and took away his files. His files! There was nothing he could do to stop them.

It could have been worse, she wanted to say, but he was on a roll, sputtering about how he called the ACLU and got a series of voice mail instructions and was put on hold. As if he had time to wait for someone.

"I call and I call, this lawyer and that one," Mr. Lao said. He jammed the elevator button with a pudgy finger. His nails were rimmed with dirt, as if he'd been working on a car, but Meriam knew Mr. Lao didn't have a car, and if he did, he wouldn't have been working on it. He had given up his car when gas prices went up and driving in the city meant regular searches, not only at the bridges and tunnels, but also at stop signs, no parking zones, and gas stations. An arbitrary pattern of disruptions designed, it seemed, to unhinge the population. Meriam could imagine Mr. Lao unhinged, a door detaching itself and crashing to the floor, crushing everything underneath it. For if he were a door, he would be steel, armor-plated even, self-protective and destructive when he came undone.

"I don't have time, I say," Mr. Lao continued. "No time to wait for someone. I need help now. They take the files and then it is too late."

His English shorthanded itself when he was stressed. The government, he claimed, had taken his files, as if it was his fault the bomb—a bomb that would not have detonated, he heard—was found in his office.

"I try to tell them, it could mean for anyone." He looked directly at Meriam, his blue eyes sharp slivers of light against his burnished skin. "Your office was my office not long time ago. Maybe bomb was meant for you."

Meriam had known people like him. Unhinged doors. Mr. Lao was a survivalist, and if this meant shifting the attention to someone else, he would not think twice. They were not in this together. They were not revolving doors or even a set of double doors, teams that worked together, even though the men who took his files would look at him, see her, and would not notice the difference.

Meriam wondered if he had said anything about her or Vijay to the investigators. Looking at his rounded profile, she thought of a line in a poem: the survivor is almost always the youngest. She always forgot the next line, but this time the words came to her in a rush, as they stepped into the elevator and the doors closed.

And you shall have to relinquish that title before long.

• • •

56

Between leaving the office and arriving at the restaurant, Meriam decided not to tell Clyde about the bomb in their building. She could not say why exactly she wanted to keep this information to herself—she had no sense of misguided loyalty toward Mr. Lao—and she told herself that nothing would come of sharing it with Clyde, so why bother? The closest he came to acknowledging the city's state of siege were the words scrawled on one of his old t-shirts: "The city is no longer on fire...but it's still burning." And this had nothing to do with their post-post 9/11 reality; it was a quote from a play or book, he said, and the shirt was a gift.

So in between the antipasto and the main course, Meriam let Clyde chatter about growing up in Bloomington, how he learned to shop for groceries for his mother, who was self-conscious about her English, the way she looked.

Meriam stopped chewing on her bread. "Wait. The way she looked?" She frowned. She had been half-listening. She thought he had grown up in New Jersey, that his mother was born and raised in Newark.

Clyde passed his hand over his head. "The hijab, man. She liked not having to worry about her hair or men looking at her."

This was new, the Muslim mother, the non-native speaker—from where, Meriam wondered, because Clyde, with his slanted wide eyes, milky brown skin, wide smile, could have been from anywhere. He walked and talked American, but he was neither black nor white, more a brown that fell between Asia and Africa.

Their dinner arrived, steaming plates of tender squid on a bed of linguine and red sauce. The waitress set the plates down heavily on the black and white checked tablecloth. She sighed and glanced around the half-empty room. This had been an expensive, tourist-friendly restaurant once, in the middle of the city. From their booth, Meriam counted seven empty booths around the room. Several years ago, the room would have been packed, and she and Clyde would still be standing outside, waiting for their table.

Before she could return to his mother, Clyde said, "Think they're going to pull Lao in? Make him sweat under a hot lamp in a dark room?"

"You know a lot for someone who hasn't been to the office in weeks," she said. She wondered if he knew about Vijay.

Clyde shrugged. "Everyone's getting all paranoid again. Looking for terrorists under their beds. The only terrorist I'm seeing is the police. Every time I see some guy in one of those windbreakers with the big yellow letters, I go in the other direction."

"What does a terrorist look like?" An image of Guy, his grinning face, all cheek and chin, snapping fingers, came to her.

Clyde grinned and shook his head.

"Not me, baby. I have no political convictions whatsoever."

He was relaxed, on his way to a party after dinner. She would remember him this way, always: Clyde with his closely cropped hair, cut like a black knit cap that hugged his shiny scalp, and his small white teeth, baby teeth arrested in development because his mother could not afford milk the year his father died, at least that was one story he told.

Meriam did not mind the stories. Theirs was a friendship based on what they did not know about each other, only hers were the sins of omission rather than commission. Unlike Clyde, she could not make things up as she went along. Her life had one draft, and this she kept to herself.

Vijay had guessed, made the connection to a family photo in one of his old clippings. He was old enough to remember reading about her grandfather. When he saw her, there was, he had said, no mistaking the profile. It belonged to kings. He kept her secret.

Now here was Clyde, mid-sentence, looking at her with uncustomary stillness. His almond eyes were unblinking, and his hand paused between his mouth and his plate.

"What," she said.

"You remind me of someone," he said, his voice arched with surprise.

She waited for him to snap his fingers, hold them to his forehead in careful recall. Her throat and mouth were dry, as if lined with old breadcrumbs. This was Clyde, her friend. This all-American Clyde, who cared nothing for history or politics, what could he know, what could he care about the world. Self-absorbed, carefree, Chameleon Clyde, Vijay called him. Clyde who would show up to work in a dress shirt and suit one day, the next in jeans and a t-shirt that showed off his biceps, the same muscles he claimed not to work on, in true, diva, superstar style.

"You remind me of my mother," he said, after a minute.

"Which one?" she asked, trying to make a joke.

The mother who wore a hijab, covered her mouth when she laughed, punished him with silence, not speaking for days when he displeased her? Or was it the Newark mother, who drank herself to sleep, yet somehow managed to make sure he got to school every day? Or some other mother, one Clyde had not invented yet?

"She used to tell me stories," Clyde said, twirling some pasta on his fork, then letting it slip to his plate. "Mostly about how she left home. All those years here, and she's still calling another country home. I couldn't figure out why she loved it so much. She ran away when she was ten, after her parents went to jail for being traitors. She ate dirt. She said she sucked on stones to keep the hunger away."

Meriam put her fork down. The food turned acid in her mouth, and she thought she might have to get up from the table, pass out in the bathroom. She willed herself to breathe.

Stories of eating dirt and sucking stones belonged to any number of exiles and refugees.

But this one reminded Clyde of Meriam. This imaginary mother.

"Where was she from?" she asked.

"I think," Clyde spoke slowly, "you are from the same country."

In the two years they had known each other, he had never asked a single question about her family, where she was from, even if she had siblings. He had asked nothing of her other than a few laughs, some collegiality. And she had expected no more from him. She did not trust him, and he did not seem to care. This was not that kind of friendship.

Meriam pushed the food around on her plate; the squid, no longer covered in sauce, looked like rubber. The pasta spun out in glutinous threads, slick with oil.

How, she wondered, could she respond without revealing the sorry story of her family, her grandfather dethroned, her parents imprisoned, the rest—aunts, uncles, cousins—executed as enemies of the state. She would then have to tell him about how she and her brother and sister hid at the ambassador's house, and then languished at a refugee camp, hiding from the new government, on a mission to destroy what remained of their family.

But maybe Clyde knew this already. Maybe his bedtime stories were about the civil war, the military coup, the summary executions. Maybe he had fallen asleep to the sound of dogs barking all night, in symphony with growling American-made tanks on late night joy rides.

As if he could no longer take the silence between them, Clyde reached into his portfolio and pulled out the cover for Kemal's book. "This will make you happy," he said, handing it to her across the table.

The illustration was bright blue with black type, with an inked drawing of what looked like the Great Wall of China, barbed wire curling like ivy about it, broken triangles of glass protruding from the top.

"I had a big 'KEEP OUT' sign in the middle, but that was kind of obvious."

"It's bright," Meriam said. "Kemal will love it."

They finished their meal, with Clyde first talking about his roommate, the flight attendant, then one of the other freelancers, then a friend who worked on the docks. His conversation, as usual, ranged over a vast landscape. But Meriam knew, as she forced herself to eat dessert, that their friendship had irrevocably changed. With the cover in hand, she would not have to see him for a while. She could farm the work out to other freelancers, put some space between them. Give him a chance to forget. No matter what he said or did, she would be looking over her shoulder, evermore cautious in her actions and words. She knew how quickly people could turn on you. Nothing like a bloody coup, she and her sister would try to joke, to teach you who your friends were.

In her haste to get away, Meriam had forgotten to give Clyde his check. So she had called him and left a message on his machine. She wanted him to come in, pick up the check. She could ask him about his mother then, see how much he really knew. Even if she wanted to send the check to him, she could not. His file was still missing, and with it, his address. She had flipped through all the files twice, and finally concluded that she was mistaken: Clyde's file had been confiscated after all, swept up in the random collection of "evidence," for whatever it was Vijay had done.

Meriam decided that when Clyde waltzed in, she would not wait for him to ask her where she was from. She would claim another country, create a different family, write herself a new history the way so many Germans, after World War II, suddenly became French or Swiss. She would tell him tribal similarities overrode national boundaries; she and his mother could be from different countries and look like sisters. Then she would give him his check and tell him there was no work right now, call later.

She was not the same person who had walked off her job a few years ago, disappeared from sight.

Or was she?

Days passed. Snow piled up along the sidewalks, plowed into huge soot-covered mountains where cars once parked. The city was broke, the salt supply was low. The snowplows worked sporadically, and still more snow fell. It seemed as if it would never stop snowing.

Meriam worked all morning, finally getting up when her back started to ache from sitting too long. But she could not avoid Mr. Lao, stationed at the elevator it seemed, whenever she left the office.

"I heard about your boss. Arrested as material witness," he said, shaking his head.

"Who told you that?" Meriam asked, staring at the shiny steel doors of the elevator. She shoved her shaking hands into her coat pockets.

"People disappear. I notice, I ask questions."

Meriam opened her purse. The answer to most things, her mother once said, might be found at the bottom of a purse. Meriam pretended to move things around, even though her keys were exactly where she had put them, in the zippered pocket, her makeup in its own bag, her wallet on one side of the divided purse, her subway map on the other. No loose tampons, shredded tissues, empty mint tins, melted lipsticks and old compacts here.

If she disappeared, what questions would Mr. Lao ask?

"What about the other guy who is all the time here? The bald one, black guy?"

Jangling her keys, Meriam said, "You go ahead without me."

"I hold the elevator."

If she ever lost the purse, the person finding it would learn little about her. There would be no pause over a scrap of paper, no attempt to make meaning of the name and number on it, no thumbing through a worn paperback to see where she'd stopped reading, what she used for a bookmark. Except for her bankcard, on which she used only her first initial, her name appeared on nothing. No old pay stubs, no library card, no driver's license. The purse was designed to be lost and never returned.

"That's okay. I'll be a while."

And she fled, ignoring his insistence, her hands shaking as she turned the key in the lock. She closed the door behind her—a flimsy, hollow door that would do no harm if it came unhinged—and leaned against it, her heart pounding, blood drumming in her ears. She finally heard the ping of the elevator. And then she heard silence, the silence of an empty office, the silence of best-laid plans quietly crashing to the floor.

Meriam's hands were clammy as she listened to the recorded voice announce that Clyde's number had been disconnected. Even if she could go to his neighborhood, find his apartment—he was ex-directory, naturally—she knew that she would find it empty. Clyde was gone, and with him, all of her questions and his answers to them.

About him, she knew—she knew precisely nothing. Mother in Newark, mother in Bloomington. African, Muslim, non-native speaker. Maybe. If she called the police, reported him missing, what would she say? He has something that belongs to me. He knows more about me than I know about him. I think. Maybe.

Whatever he knew, Clyde did not know that she had once held a gun to her younger brother's head. When they came home that day, found chairs overturned and their mother's clothes spilling out of the closet, she and her two siblings hid behind the desk in her father's library, listened to the sound of gunfire, and waited for the men to come back.

"It's the sound of two hands clapping," she had told Vijay. "Sharp claps, followed by silence."

He nodded; the sound of gunfire was hard to forget. He was in his sixties, with thick white hair that reached his collar. They were drinking tea; it was a slow afternoon, and they were between issues. He had rummaged about, found the tea bags, sugar, powdered milk. Somehow he always managed to get the powder to dissolve. When she tried, it turned into watery clumps. Refugee blend, she called it, powdered milk in weak, watery tea. Vijay used extra tea bags, and when he made tea, she could forget the past momentarily, pretend the milk was real.

Whatever Clyde knew, he did not hear her tell Vijay about the pearl-handled gun she pulled from her mother's drawer, and how she promised herself that the moment they saw dust behind the palm trees lining the driveway, she would shoot her brother, shoot her sister, shoot herself. She was fourteen, the middle child, stuck between her sniveling eight-year-old brother and her dumbstruck older sister. She was the emperor's granddaughter; she would not be taken prisoner.

What had Vijay said? The habit of fear is hard to break.

Whatever Clyde knew about her, he did not know what stopped her: the chop-chop of a helicopter, startling her so that she forgot the gun in her hand just long enough to see the ambassador, the tails of his tuxedo flapping as he alighted on to the driveway.

Whatever Clyde had, he did not have dogs baying through the night, the cold click of the safety in her hand, her brother's tuneless humming, her sister's asthmatic gasping. He did not have the smell of blood mingled with dust, the acrid smell of young eucalyptus trees burning, the sharpness of creosote and kerosene in a hot sun.

They had changed their names and invented lives that relied on half-truths: a paraplegic uncle in London (truth), parents killed in a car accident in Paris (false). They kept away from other expats, avoided social clubs, cultural events, places where they might run into people who knew their family. Their uncle, an unhappy man suddenly saddled with three unhappy children, told them that many people had suffered during their grandfather's reign, and they would avenge themselves on his descendants. Twenty years later, fact and fiction were a seamless fabric.

Whatever Clyde knew, he did not know her. Neither had Guy. She held the Sheraton ashtray in her hands, cold comfort in its weight. They did not know how one day she sat in the coffee shop that faced the water and watched the wind whip across it and the rain-slicked streets of Copenhagen. They did not know the pleasure of sitting still in a storm, how fine it was at that moment, her anonymity complete.

All substance, no form. Meriam set the plain ashtray back on her desk and riffled through the files in the long cabinet against the wall. It rattled, and the paper felt sharp against her dry fingers. What burning city did his shirt refer to? Was his roommate really a flight attendant? Had he been here the day the bomb was found in Mr. Lao's office, a face in the crowd, watching the police evacuate the building?

When Meriam tried to hold Clyde, see him fully and completely, he melted, slipped through her fingers like water.

She kicked the file drawer closed, rubbed her hands on her jeans. When she left her last job, she did not think to go to Human Resources, take her personnel file. When she left her father's library, she grabbed her sister's hand, her brother's hand. She could not then or now remember what she did with the gun. And when the helicopter hovered over what had been their home, she did not look down or back.

She had underestimated him. Or, rather, mis-estimated. Where there was no trust, there could be no friendship. On her desk, a stack of files. She could sort through them one more time. She put her fingers on her temples; her stomach growled. Weak afternoon sun filtered in through the blinds, long thin fingers across the industrial carpet.

The week before he was arrested, Vijay had said to her, "If something happens to me, just carry on. Make sure you get Kemal's book out."

Meriam picked up the files, rapidly replaced them in the file cabinet. She kicked the cabinet again, a dull thud of leather against metal. She locked it, with keys neither she nor Vijay ever used. The small brassy keys felt heavy in her hand; they were identical, on a thin metal ring. The black cabinet sat in front of her, unmoved, unchanged by the single key in its lock. She unlocked it and put the keys in her desk drawer.

If she left now, she would always be leaving.

Meriam slid into her coat, listening for the sound of Mr. Lao by the elevator. The habit of fear.

This time, it was Clyde who had left. Clyde who hated snow.

Perhaps that was all she needed.

There was more snow forecast tonight. Meriam smiled. She would leave work early, watch the children slide down the big hill near her house, catch a few flakes on her tongue. She would feel the snow melt on her face. After the screams of the children playing subsided and night fell, she would walk home, call her sister in London. Tomorrow, she would be back.

And there would be Mr. Lao, by the elevator. And she would ask him, Now, tell me, what exactly is your business?

# Flight Attendants Take Your Seats

When the American military jet took off, the sound filled the empty skies and reverberated through the city. In the seminar room at the Gander Aviation Training Institute, the table shook, the students grabbed their plastic cups of iced water, their notebooks, their reading glasses. The take-offs were sporadic, and each one was a surprise. The room, a carpeted, windowless cave, looked like it would be soundproofed, but it was not.

"The average flight attendant does not improve flight by flight," Valerie said. She had short poufy blond hair and zero sense of humor. "Right, Alex?"

Alex was under the table looking for his pen. He sat up quickly. Ignoring his spinning head, he whispered to his neighbor John, "Lend me a pencil." Valerie had already interrupted herself twice to ask him a question, which he had answered correctly. But he knew she didn't take him seriously, and he wanted to prove she was wrong. He was paying attention; he would graduate at the top of this class. He would be her first choice for one of the two coveted internships. Flying colors, no pun intended, he had told John the night before. Some of their classmates didn't even have a bachelor's degree. Valerie herself had gone straight from high school to a job at one of the major airlines—she refused to say which one. Surely he, Alex, was smarter than an aging stewardess with secretary hair.

"Use the word 'stewardess' in front of her," John said, "and you'll be going home on the first flight out of here."

"I was being ironic," Alex said. He didn't expect John to understand. He was too old for a start, nearly fifty. And he was American. With his droopy eyes, long face and deep voice, he looked and sounded like Eeyore.

"You have to be prepared for plateaus. It is during one of these plateaus that you will have to deploy your best serving skills—holding a cup of Diet Coke without spilling it on 3C while you reach across for 3A.

"If you're in first class or on an international flight, it will have to be a steady hand pouring that wine. Not to mention the after dinner coffee and tea." Valerie looked at the twenty people sitting at the table and blinked. She blinked often and slowly, like a doll, and it was unclear if this was for emphasis or because she had dry eyes.

"Nothing beats practice," Valerie said.

The institute was in a strip mall not far from the Gander International Airport. The month-long course was guaranteed to prepare its students for the highly competitive airline interview. The only guarantee of getting a job, however, was one of the two internships at an unnamed airline; according to the institute's brochure, interns always went on to well-paid corporate jobs. No messing around in the commercial sector, cleaning up vomit on the Dubuque to Albuquerque route. Private jets, well-heeled clients, exotic destinations—that's what the students sitting at the long oval table wanted. They followed Valerie's PowerPoint presentation closely, most of them taking notes, even though she had given them a thick manual to study in the evenings. Two internships, twenty students. The math was inescapable.

"Improvement," Valerie droned on. "Improvement comes in plateaus. A flight attendant who services an entire 747 cabin in 30 minutes does not see that time drop slowly to 29 minutes, then 28, then 27. Instead the 30 suddenly drops to 25. And then, overnight, the 25 minutes will become 17."

"Thirty minutes to serve coffee to Tom Cruise," Shelly whispered to Alex. She was a housewife with nearly grown children, and she wanted to see the world on a private jet. It didn't matter whose; if not a celebrity, a corporation would do.

"She'll probably end up on the Columbus to Des Moines route. On Southwest," John whispered on Alex's other side.

John worked for a software company and had been living on an island in the Puget Sound before his wife kicked him out, telling him to get his "droopy ass in gear and get a life." He had thick gray hair and spoke slowly, which gave him the appearance of being sensitive. Already two women had asked him out. But because he did not quite understand the status of his marriage—had his wife booted him permanently or just until he got better?—he agonized about the two women and went out with neither, sticking close to Alex instead.

"The key," Valerie continued, clicking to the next slide, "is efficiency. Especially on those short haul flights." Behind her, on the screen, the word "efficiency" appeared in bold blue letters, pulsing to some internal rhythm.

"You can't even get a direct flight to Gander anymore," John muttered. "How's that for efficiency?" He was still traumatized by his flight to St. John's, which required three stops, including an overnight layover at the Detroit Airport.

Alex wanted to be efficient. He wanted to leave St. Catharines behind and fly the friendly skies. Inefficiency, that was his friend Arthur, already married, with three kids, not yet twenty-five, and their buddy Red Dog, mean and drunk, also not yet twenty-five. Red Puppy, two years younger than the Dog, was the closest to competent, and he had just been fired from Kimberly-Clark. When they were boys, the stench from the paper mill used to fill the town on hot summer days, and now when they gathered, the friends talked about those days like old men. They reminisced about late nights and trips across the border to Buffalo with a full car and two guys stuffed in the trunk. Now they needed passports to go south, and anyway, only Alex and Red Puppy had a chance of fitting into the trunk of a car. To Alex, they looked and sounded like old men, and with them, Alex felt old, as if he were in fact married with two kids.

After dinner that night, Alex, John, and Shelly sat at the bar at the Albatross Hotel, where Alex and John, the only men in the program, were sharing a room. The bar was quiet. Fake fishing nets and plastic lobsters hung from the crown molding. They were drinking Screech, the local brew.

"Why doesn't Valerie tell us who she used to work for?" Shelly crunched on some ice from her glass of water. "What's she hiding?"

"She probably worked the Pittsburgh to Columbus to Pittsburgh to Orlando route," Alex said. "Nothing glamorous about that."

"Oh you," Shelly said. "So young, so innocent."

She was tipsy. Alex had no idea what she was talking about.

"We're all going to end up on that route," John said, peering into his empty glass.

"Don't be funny," Shelly said, putting her hand on John's arm. She sat between them, and Alex wondered if she was one of the women John had rejected. With her blond shoulder-length hair and a smattering of freckles across her nose, she was not unattractive—for an older woman. When she heard he was twenty-four, she took Alex's chin in her hand and said, "Lucky boy. You have your whole life before you." Alex also had all his hair, thick and brown, and what his girlfriend Jocelyn called soulful eyes. Soulful and young, that was Alex, but neither trait was enough to get him out of St. Catharines and into the world.

"I wonder if the practical's tomorrow," John said. "We're the only ones in the bar."

John was right; except for the couple sitting in a booth playing cards, there was no one else in the bar. No one wanted to take a chance, be less alert or late for the big day—to do poorly on the practical would be tantamount to failing the course. Valerie would not tell them the date of the flight simulator trials, but since this was the last week, that day could be any day. They didn't know what the flight simulator entailed exactly, only that it was the practical.

"Another round?" Shelly asked.

"I'll pass," Alex said.

The Screech tasted like burnt sugar. After one glass, Alex had a mild buzz going, and any more alcohol would bring on the head spins. He was a lightweight among his friends, unable to drink much because of a vestibular disorder that affected his balance and sometimes left him in bed for a week, with vertigo and nausea. He had a history of motion sickness, something he had deliberately left off his information sheet. He could fly, as long as he took Dramamine; he could stay awake, as long as he followed the Dramamine with several cups of coffee. But he found that Dramamine did not allow him to drink more, and this made him a loser among his friends, and a real catch among Jocelyn's friends because he never got drunk.

"I think it's great you majored in English," Shelly said. "I used to keep a journal before I got married."

"You used to do a lot of things before you got married," Alex said. She had alluded to long distance running, a career, travel. On the eve of a long-awaited trip to London, her boyfriend since high school had finally proposed; the trip, a three-month corporate exchange program, ended a month later, when Shelly returned home to be fitted for her wedding dress and stayed.

"You wouldn't understand," John said. "Marriage changes everything."

It was Jocelyn's talk of wedding dresses and rings that had prompted Alex to send off his application to Gander. Distant and remote, Newfoundland—New-Found-Land— had promise and potential, despite all the Newfie jokes that surfaced when he told everyone his plan. Jocelyn, forever the optimist, was disturbingly happy. "I hear family members can travel for free," she'd said. Like Shelly, she wore her blond hair shoulder length. The similarity ended there, though. Unlike Shelly, who dressed quietly in khakis and cords, Jocelyn imagined herself some kind of Stevie Nicks. She wore flowing skirts, lacy knit shawls, and a stack of bracelets along her arm that clattered when she moved. Because she worked in a bookstore, she had to dress the part.

"But it's a corporation," Alex had argued.

"Don't be a purist."

"I just don't see how candles and soap belong in a bookstore."

"People like to read in the bath," Jocelyn said, and Alex was struck once again by how he felt like he'd landed from another planet. Since returning home after graduation, every move he made felt wrong. At work, when Red Dog dropped a pallet of beer, Alex had to twist his face and swallow hard to repress the hysterical laughter. Four years of college, and here he was, back at Molson with Red Dog, fishing through broken glass for the one bottle that may have survived.

The next day, after a brief lecture on life vests, Valerie led the group up a flight of stairs to a room that looked like a gym, large and full of equipment Alex didn't recognize. In the middle of the room sat a platform with five rows of seats, with a scattering of mannequins sitting in them. They were all female. Some were naked, some were dressed, and as the class walked around the platform, Alex could see that each mannequin had the same blank face, the same stiff helmet hair, the same chipped fingernails. They shared the glassy faraway look of the dead. Just looking at them made him feel queasy.

"Remember, folks," Valerie was saying. "You won't improve drink by drink. It's a cluster of movements that will suddenly come together as your inner ear adjusts to the balance."

Some people with vestibular disorders experienced them as fullness in the head; others, like Alex, had to cope with nausea, vertigo, and a lack of balance. When the clinic that diagnosed him gave Alex a sheet of exercises to correct his "disorder," he shoved it into his schoolbag and left it there until the end of term. He was too young to have a disorder. Disorders got you kicked out of the pack. Disorders were for rich people, people who could afford to stay in bed all day. If he went home and told his father he had a disorder, his father would say, "Something you got in college?"

Alex was fifth in line, between Shelly and John. Every morning for the past three weeks, he had been taking Dramamine in preparation for the practical. This morning, though, he'd woken up late and forgot his pill. Just watching the platform rock, roll, then shudder made him feel sick.

His father used to say Alex could get sick on a bicycle. His older sister, Sarah, who worked at a health food store in Ottawa, had sent him remedies: ginger capsules, peppermint tea, homeopathy, sea bands, essential oils. When nothing worked, she told him over the phone he needed to be de-fragged. She was ten years older than Alex and was used to him accepting everything she said. But he'd been to college—more than she or their older brother Hugh had ever done—and neither of them seemed that smart to him anymore.

"De-frag? As in de-fragmentation? Or defragging a computer?"

"De-frag," Sarah repeated, like he was a five-year-old kid and still believed beer was a magic potion only witches and warlocks could drink.

But now, watching Alyson walk down the aisle, her face tight with concentration as Valerie made the platform sway and shift, Alex thought about de-frag with regret. At the Clinic for Vestibular Disorders they had told him he couldn't expect a cure, only a decrease in symptoms. He did the exercises for a month then gave up because they made him more nauseous.

"Watch how Alyson bends at the knees," Valerie said. "See? Not a drop spilled. And now she'll go through, collect the trash, and boom—she's done."

Valerie clicked her stopwatch, wrote something down on her plastic clipboard. John had stolen a look at the back of it and told Alex it was a pharmaceutical ad for TB medication.

"Who gets TB anymore?" John asked.

"People," Alex said. He was too tired to explain that while John had been hiding on his island, TB had made a comeback, especially among the poor.

Now it was Shelly's turn. She smiled, but her hands shook, and then she spilled a drink when the platform dipped to one side. Valerie wrote something down.

"And boom," John whispered. "The plane goes down. Because Shelly spilled some OJ on 3A."

Valerie said nothing when Shelly fell into a mannequin's lap, one with no clothes sitting in 5C, and when Shelly was done, none of the class looked at her. Mistakes were infectious, the airlines unforgiving. Valerie had already dismissed two people for being late to class. "An airplane waits for no one, and neither do I," she said.

When Alex had refused to go to Ottawa for de-frag, Sarah said, "The problem is you really don't want to leave St. Catharines. You still think mommy's coming home."

His mother, a flight attendant for Air Canada until she married, had left when Alex was four. All that remained of her was a red and white uniform, a cancelled passport, and a pile of unlabelled photographs, some of them discolored Polaroids with color bleeding into the white edges.

Alex didn't want to think about his mother. He stood by the galley and nodded at Valerie. The platform started to undulate gently, and he unlatched the cart and pushed it down the aisle. So far, so good. He showed 1A how to access the tray and then he put some peanuts and a plastic cup of Coke on it. Was he supposed to leave the whole can? Or was this an airline that cheaped out on soft drinks and split the cans between passengers?

"People are getting restless, Alex," Valerie said. "They want their drink before they land, not after."

When Alex told his friends he was getting a degree in English, Red Puppy had asked, "So what do you do? Sit around and read books all day?"

You couldn't get nauseated reading. One of his advisors had suggested graduate school, but Alex didn't think he could take another five years of being mocked by his father and friends. At least if he were flying, he could put some distance between himself and the gay jokes.

The plane tilted, and Alex's stomach went with it. Bile rose in his throat, and he grabbed the cart. Think of something else. He timed his breaths: YYZ, Toronto; YHF, Halifax; YQZ, St. John's; YQX, Gander.

"Sometimes," Valerie was saying, "your inner ear will go out of whack and the nausea will grab you. It gets worse with each flight and then one day—boom—you won't notice it anymore. As long as you don't throw up, you'll be fine."

Alex gave the mannequin in the Girl Scout uniform a Diet Coke. The embroidered patches on her vest were frayed, and the sleeve of her blue shirt was torn. One more row, and he'd be done. A quick clean up, and then—

The plane dipped sharply, and the cart began to roll away from him. He braced his legs and clung to it, wondering what point Valerie was trying to prove. Maybe she had marked him as the runt of the litter. With only two internships, she had to weed out the losers any way she could.

Suddenly there was no movement. The platform had stopped. The plastic cups had toppled over, spilling across the trays and people. The drinks were all water; it would dry and leave no stain on the worn seats and the semi-dressed mannequins.

"Not bad, Alex," Valerie said. "You put the passengers first, kept them safe. Can't have a cart rolling all over them." She looked at her clipboard and chewed on the end of her pen before writing something down.

Alex reached for the white bag in the seat pocket and threw up.

In the afternoon, Alex and John went to the airport to watch planes land and take off.

"Tough break," John said finally, as they scanned the empty arrivals hall. It was overwhelmingly brown and orange, with only two baggage carousels.

"Are you sure this is it?" Alex had expected the "crossroads of the world" to be bustling with people. The airport in Hamilton was busier than this.

He knew he had scored highest on the written exams and was the best on emergency and safety protocols—a peek at Valerie's TB clipboard had revealed that—so maybe he could make up for today's performance later in the week during the mock interview. He would tell Valerie it was food poisoning.

The day was cold and drizzly. In St. Catharines, the tulips and daffodils would be out, but May in Newfoundland meant patches of snow under the trees and a bone chilling cold when it rained. Alex and John ate peanut butter sandwiches in the car and waited for the chartered flights to land. By three, only one freight had touched down—no Tom Cruise, no Paris Hilton. Just a few pallets of what looked like old clothes.

"Probably on their way to Africa," John said. "Refugee camps."

When Alex had told his father about Gander, his father put down his racing form and said, "You'll be a waitress in the air, only without the tips, and you'll have to mop up puke and everyone will pinch your ass."

His father leaned back into his recliner and stared at the ticker tape on TV. He had lost $5000 on a stock tip from a friend, but he still liked to watch the tape, as if he understood and was not just a salesman at the Rent-and-Roll.

"You're not, are you?" he asked during a commercial.

"No, dad," Alex said. "I'm not gay."

And that had been it. If Alex had thought his father would say something about his mother—how nothing was ever good enough for her, how flying had spoiled her for an ordinary life—he would have been disappointed. But he knew his father had buried his mother the day after she took off for good, and there was no point talking about the dead. The two older children had left a long time ago—Sarah to Ottawa, Hugh out west, where he worked in trucking—and their father had run out of arguments to keep Alex at home.

"My wife called today," John said. "She doesn't want me to come home. Says she enjoys listening to NPR in the morning by herself."

They watched the plane taxi down the runway then lift into the air, a gray cigar snuffed out by the clouds.

"Do you want to go home?" Alex asked.

"I was thinking I'd head over to Bonavista after the class ends and take one of those puffin tours," John said.

Alex did not want to go home. He didn't know what he wanted to do, but he knew he did not want to return to St. Catharines. He would never work in a bookstore. He did not want to end up like Shelly, middle-aged and looking for a second chance. Or like John, gloomy and dream-less. Or his father, bitter and resigned.

Alex reached for another sandwich and handed half to John.

"They call puffins PPF's," John said. "Piss Poor Flyers. They go so far, and then they drop like a stone."

"I suppose that's what Valerie wrote next to my name." Alex leaned back in his seat and closed his eyes.

"Some people really need this job. They're not getting a second chance."

"At least Shelly can go home."

"Have a heart," John said. "This is it for her. She's not twenty-four with her whole life ahead of her. This counts."

Alex found it hard to believe that Gander once counted. When it was completed in the early 1960s, the airport was crucial to refueling transatlantic flights. Then came 747s, non-stop flights, and suddenly air travel had outgrown the airport. It was a ghost town, a relic from another time, the last stop before giving up.

"What do you want to do, Alex?" John asked. He rubbed his eyes and blinked, as if he were holding back tears. John and his wife had never had kids, and John was sure this was the reason for his wife's unhappiness. The reason for his unhappiness remained unspoken.

"I can't go to graduate school," Alex said.

"I read somewhere that people with severe motion sickness are also prone to agoraphobia," John said. "The illness becomes a way for them to never leave home."

Alex frowned. John was starting to sound like Sarah. "I damaged my inner ear. Nothing psychological about that."

John smiled. "I'd pay good money to watch you puke on a passenger. Anyway, you can still go for an interview, on your own. You don't need Val's seal of approval to do it."

Had his mother flown through Gander? Alex desperately wanted to know. Sarah said their mother had tried hard to stay grounded. Alex, the afterthought baby, had been part of that effort. "But she was an Aquarius," Sarah said. "Born to travel the world and meet new people. We were never going to be enough for her." When she died in Bali two years ago, he didn't know how to feel. Now he wanted to ask his mother how she could leave everything behind—her friends, family, her children. Maybe by the time she realized what she had done, it was too late to return.

The cost of a dream was an empty airfield and the sound of windsocks flapping in the air. Someone was always getting left behind, or dropping mid-flight into the ocean. Alex wondered if Red Dog, Arthur, Jocelyn, his father would stand on the tarmac and wave goodbye. Or would they forget him, the way people did before air travel, when leaving home was a more finite proposition?

Alex and John sat in the car for a long time, watching the gray tarmac, waiting for another plane to land. They waited until it was dark, and still no plane landed. And in the morning, when they hit the road in John's rental car, cumulus clouds clotted the blue sky, not a single plane in sight.

# Foreign Relations

If asked, Meena wouldn't have said she followed him to the store, trailed him like a bloodhound after a fox, sniffing the air for the scent and taste of him. No, that wasn't the way she remembered it. What happened—history as she remembered it—was that she saw him riding his bike, his precious titanium mountain bike, in the direction of the Stop & Shop at the end of King Street. She had been planning to go there anyway, and as she came out of the Dunkin' Donuts she saw him ride past. He was wearing his black wraparound sunglasses and worn topsiders with no socks, though the temperature had plummeted the night before, turning the islands of grass in the sidewalk into stiff frozen needles that crunched underfoot.

And no, she wouldn't have been able to tell anyone—not even herself—how she came to know his bicycle was precious or that it was a mountain bike or that it was titanium. How she came by the details of this man with green eyes and a coarse blond ponytail was a mystery to her. She didn't realize she had them, carried them around in the back pocket of her jeans like forgotten tissues and old grocery lists that shredded in the wash and attached themselves to every other piece of clothing in the load. These details clung like the pills on a cheap sweater that multiplied on their own. They were part of her now, useless details that offered no insight as to why Larry had disappeared in the middle of his first year at the hospital. About him, she thought she knew what everyone else knew, threadbare scraps: Mayflower descendant; son of a famous New York district judge; Harvard graduate; one year of law school; a broken heart, maybe two (his or someone else's?); several step-families; and a passion for the outdoors. He skied and backpacked in remote areas of the world. He enjoyed skydiving, hang gliding, and kayaking in white water. Mostly, though, he climbed mountains, and his skin was always tanned, ruddy from a life lived close to nature. When she thought of America, the image of Larry floated by, next to billboards for the Marlboro man and Coca Cola.

Her skin was also tan, but she'd been born with it, and was often mistaken for a Seminole Indian in Florida where her parents had moved after one harsh New York winter. "East Indian," she learned to call herself, but the blank eyes of her classmates made her wish she could say Seminole, Apache, Cherokee—something they'd at least seen on TV and could believe existed. And later, as she grew up, it was elephants and maharajahs and poverty she had to explain to her classmates at the New England boarding school her parents sent her to. Six years passed and then she stayed for college and med school. Unlike her tropical parents, she had learned to love the crisp winter air, the peculiar light that deadened the earth just before snow fell from the sky. Loving the cold was different from being cold. Accordingly, she loved the accoutrements of the cold: nubby wool sweaters, thick black tights, long sleeves, high necks, fingerless gloves, and sheepskin slippers. She bought heavy socks and turtlenecks and leggings in catalogue colors of summer—fuchsia, harvest green, and lapis lazuli.

Long distance, aunties in Delhi worried about finding the right man for her, living as she did in a small, no-name valley town, with such weather. Meena never mentioned the hot, humid summers, or the beauty of the crocuses and daffodils in the spring, or even the celebrated fall foliage that attracted caravans of cars with out-of-state license plates. She wrote to her aunts infrequently; they could easily think she lived in a place where it was winter all the time, and she let them because she didn't want them to find her a husband.

She could articulate this, if asked, but several years would pass before she'd be able to see how her love for the cold made her follow her former colleague into the grocery store. She would remember her actions, but she would be unable to assign motivation, emotion, or intent to them. She remembered the ache in her fingers, stiff from cigarettes and lack of sleep. She was in the store, she told herself, because Anita was having a potluck that night, and she had to make chicken curry.

She was using a recipe from a book her mother had sent her a year ago, with an admonishment inscribed on the flyleaf. "You must eat, bacchi. Even doctors get sick." If only her mother knew. Eating would not cure her illness. She would need a soul transplant, a new resident to occupy her body, to get this sickness out of it. She couldn't name it, but she knew she had it. If not, why was she tracking Larry in a grocery store?

She panicked for a moment when she thought she'd lost him between the meat and dairy cases, but the store was nearly empty, and she found him easily around the corner, near the cookies. She watched him from the end of the aisle. He read the package in his hand, holding it close to his face, his sunglasses now perched on the top of his head. She remembered seeing him in round wire-rimmed glasses that slipped down his nose when he was concentrating. He threw a pack of fruit bars into his cart, and she followed him to checkout. Only two lanes were open, so she stood behind him and waited.

She had no plan. She told herself to expect nothing; meanwhile, she hoped he'd turn around. She told herself it didn't matter if he didn't apologize for yesterday. Perhaps all she wanted was for him to recognize her, and in so doing, make everything between them right again. She stared at the red reindeer in his gray Icelandic sweater and then watched his chapped hands move his groceries from cart to conveyor belt. They were dirty—no longer the hands of a practicing doctor— with scabs forming on the knuckles, ugly red scarabs of pain.

Meena pushed her cart forward, nudging the heels of his hiking boots gently.

"Sorry," she said, automatically.

He turned around and looked down at her for a second, though he was only a few inches taller than her. The skin around his eyes was crinkled, and his lips were narrow, unsmiling and tense. She thought he looked old to be a resident, and then another one of those details—the ones she stored but had no file for—came back to her. He'd traveled for a few years after college, working his way from one city to the next, always outdoors, always on the move. He had seen the world, people and places the rest of them—saddled with exams and debts— could only dream about.

Larry turned his attention back to his groceries, his marble eyes running over her without a hint of recognition. Meena felt herself blush. She touched her cheeks with icy fingertips and bent her head, hiding her face behind a curtain of thick black hair. The groceries tumbled from her hands to the belt, and she didn't look up again until she was sure he was gone.

How had she come to follow a man who would hardly look at her? She didn't know anymore; she felt she was watching herself from some great distance, a relative of the patient on the operating table, watching from the booth, unable to comprehend the action below.

The day before she'd gone straight from her shift to the gas station, exhausted and feeling ill-defined, like an out-of-focus photograph. She slouched against the car, waiting for the gas tank to fill up, and ignored the cold biting at her fingers and running up her sleeves and around her back through her unbuttoned coat. Across the street, Larry rode his bike on the sidewalk. He wasn't wearing a hat or scarf, and his hair gleamed like polished kernels of summer corn in the weak afternoon sun.

She hadn't seen him since he'd quit work three weeks ago, abruptly and with no apparent reason. She noticed he was gone when she walked into the cafeteria one day and saw that his usual table was empty. He'd never been on one of her rotations, yet she'd seen him enough to nod when they passed each other in the halls. Once she'd sat next to him at the bar, their backs to each other as they chatted with friends at opposite ends of the same table. She hardly looked at him that night, yet she remembered the black t-shirt and the golden hairs on his arm that glistened in the warm light from the candle on the table.

And now here he was. She stared at him through her eyelashes as if they were a protective screen. Her heart started racing, though if asked how she felt she would leave this detail out, deny the dry mouth and tingling at the base of her throat, the way her lips pulled against her teeth. She watched him, willed him to look over her way and talk to her. And when he crossed the street, she held her breath as he wheeled the bike towards her, and let it go when she saw him put a quarter in the air pump. He bent over the front tire, concentrating on it as if no one and nothing around him existed.

Meena got into her car and left the gas station. She would say she wasn't thinking of him when she turned right instead of left, but she'd remember the thump on the side of the car and her fear that she'd hit a pedestrian or a dog. She pulled over, and as she undid her seatbelt, she noticed Larry at the passenger door. He had taken his sunglasses off, and the lightness of his eyes and hair pierced the gloom of the car.

She opened the window. "Are you all right?" He seemed okay. She thought she'd offer him a ride home or invite him for coffee at the diner across the street.

"Where the hell did you learn to drive? Afghanistan?"

Meena stared at him, waiting for the joke. He frowned.

"Really," he said. "You should take some local driving lessons. We have laws in this country about hitting people with your car. Understand?"

The smile inside her died. "I'm sorry." But Larry was gone before the words had left her mouth.

She drove on, her eyes smarting from the cold air that whipped through the open window. Her fingers clenched the steering wheel. She'd had one real accident before, a fender bender when her car slid across an icy street and into another car. That driver apologized for the weather. He offered her a few hints about driving in the snow, after taking her insurance number, and said, "Don't let the weather make you a prisoner. You keep trying."

She was twenty, and if he was patronizing, she preferred that to hostility. She wondered where Larry thought she'd come from and why he thought it. She didn't ask herself—for she couldn't at the time—why it mattered so much.

• • •

Yet when she saw him at the grocery store the next day, she followed him, and when she saw him later that night at Anita's party, she stood near him and waited. She listened to him talk about an ice climbing expedition he'd guided last year. He had a captive audience, his usual crowd, plus some. His stories, she noticed, had an arcane quality to them, full of technical terms about ice and rock. The language, the knowledge it implied, formed a protective shield around him and his comrades, those who not only loved the cold but owned it as well.

Meena wandered into the kitchen and told Anita what had happened at the gas station. She left out the details of her morning trip to the store. For the sake of time, she told herself, unwilling to reveal what she didn't understand.

"So he thinks you're a foreigner," Anita said, as she moved between the counter and the stove, her sandals smacking the linoleum. Indoors, she always wore sandals with her salwar kameez; outdoors, she stomped around in thick-soled black boots, her one concession to American weather.

"He looked at me like I was a stranger." Meena dug her hand into her jeans pocket and looked down at Anita's red painted toenails.

"And so? He's not at the hospital anymore. You don't need to know each other. You can be strangers."

Meena envied her. Anita couldn't care, wouldn't be able to care until she'd been in this country for so long that it became home and going back to India was no longer an option. As long as she had one foot on the plane, though, she could change the subject, talk about the engineer her parents wanted her to marry and the job waiting for her at Breach Candy Hospital in Bombay. Against such rock solid tomorrows, Larry was nothing more than a temporary condition, irritating, like a mosquito bite.

• • •

After this, when Meena thought of Larry, a sick taste filled her mouth, the tannic acid of too much tea on an empty stomach or stale coffee at the end of a long day. Worse, however, she was still looking for him, waiting for him to appear and apologize. The days lurched forward, and October melted into November without her noticing. She worked with an intensity she hadn't felt before. Her eyes burned with exhaustion, and her bones buckled under an invisible weight. She took extra shifts. If she needed to prove anything to anyone, it was to herself.

Meanwhile, the aunties ignored her lack of interest in their matchmaking efforts, and the letters kept coming. In spite of herself, Meena read them, curious about the eligible "boys"—boys, still, though they were in their late twenties and early thirties—who wrote to her. The letters were impersonal, generic and tired; they were "from good families," families with money and names that meant something back in India. Names that meant nothing to her, born and bred in the New World where such things weren't supposed to matter. But in a match among strangers, a good family, height, fair skin, and a lot of money were important. These were the details that impressed.

Meena imagined her future mother-in-law running a finger across the kitchen counter, sniffing at the pile of newspapers in the corner of her living room, the mattress on the floor of the bedroom, and the half empty boxes of books and clothes, arranged like the display at a badly organized garage sale. She would notice, this fictional mother-in-law-to-be, the half empty vodka bottle, the dirty dishes, and overflowing ashtrays scattered through the small apartment. She would see, finally, dark skin, thick black hair unfashionably braided down the back, and faded jeans that hung loosely at the hips. She would notice all these things and draw conclusions about this completely unsuitable girl.

The men who wrote to Meena wanted a girl with a career. They also wanted a girl who could cook and clean and give birth to the requisite boy child to carry on the family name. Most of all—and what did it mean that these were the only men the aunties could find?—they wanted a girl who could get them a green card.

They didn't want a woman who stood in the snow, face turned to the sky to catch the fast falling flakes. They didn't want a woman who didn't button her coat on the bleakest days of the year when the landscape looked like a black and white photograph because the cold reminded her that she was still alive. They especially didn't want a woman who looked with longing at men she couldn't have. So Meena wrote back to the aunties, told them again that she was a long way from finishing school and that she wouldn't be too old when the time finally came to look for a husband. Things are different here, she told them. Girls can wait before settling down.

One night, a five-year-old boy with a cut in his scalp appeared in the emergency room. When Meena got to him, he was lying on the table, face down, crying softly. His mother held his hand and tried to calm him down. She was one of those women who'd had children too young; her face was a series of lines under cheap, cakey make-up, and her hair was lank and pale on her shoulders. She wore old acid-washed jeans, and she smelled of tobacco.

"How did it happen?" Meena asked, as she cleaned the wound. The deep cut was neat with no ragged edges of skin to force together.

"He wanted to fly," the mother said, "pretend he was at Disney World." Her blue eyes were wide as she explained how her son put a shallow box on the coffee table and tried to jump from it to the couch, about two feet away. "So, I'm hollering and hollering for him to get down, but before I can move, the box just slips and his head smacks the table. Right, bub?" She stroked her son's forehead with a small, dry hand.

After Meena had given the boy five stitches, she sent the mother out for coffee. She looked over the boy's thin body, raising his arms and listening to his heart, and casually asked him about the table he slipped on.

"Momma told me not to," he said, his lower lip sticking out. His face was tearstained, and his Aran sweater was thick and warm, frayed at the cuffs. There was no sign of any other injury on his body. "I had a lot of blood. Did my brains come out?"

Meena shook her head and smiled. "Not a single cell."

She thought about his mother, who had left the room easily, with no apparent concern for what her son might say, for what his body might reveal. She fit the profile of an abuser or someone living with one—young, on public assistance, single. But Meena had lost her trust in such details, details that looked convincing on paper and then faded in the light of the physical person behind them. She thought about how impressed the aunties would have been with Larry's pedigree, his multiple stepfamilies and his lack of professional fortitude overshadowed by his father's brilliance and his great-great-grandfather's wealth. A boy from this family couldn't be bad, they would say, poring over the horoscope for some sign, a moon or a star indicating that he could change, that he could be the person he should be.

Meena watched the mother zip up her son's jacket and gather him in her arms. The boy had recovered enough to give her a sleepy smile, and he waved goodbye as his mother carried him out.

"Thanks, doc," the woman said.

"I'm going to Disney World. I'm gonna fly. . . " the boy sang, his high-pitched voice drifting down the corridor.

• • •

And there was Larry, at the end of the long white corridor, talking animatedly to Anita. As Meena approached them, he looked up, his eyes bright and alert behind his glasses.

"The kid looked pretty happy," he said.

"He's forgotten what happened. He still thinks he's going to fly."

"Maybe he will."

She couldn't believe she was talking to him, smiling, acting as if nothing had happened. She was numb, as if she'd swallowed a load of painkillers. Or maybe just dumb enough to still care what he thought.

"Larry's going to Srinagar in December," Anita said.

Meena thought about the Hindu refugees and the European hostages, four still missing after two years, a fifth one dead, long forgotten by the front page. The husband of one of her aunties had a house in Kashmir that he never expected to see again. Neither did his children.

"They say it's safe," Larry said.

"Isn't it closed to tourists?" She looked at Anita for confirmation, but Anita ignored her.

"I'm not exactly a tourist."

Perhaps it was the way he looked over his glasses, down his nose. Perhaps it was the way he leaned against the wall, his arms by his side, and smiled as if they were friends and her approval was a forgone conclusion. Later, she would wonder what it was exactly, at that moment, and not any of the others, that made her say, "Let me tell you a story."

The aunties used to tell stories about entire villages colonized by young, drugged-out Americans and Europeans. "These people," Auntie would say, spitting the words. "No one asked them to come here. They took over that one village. In the end, only one budhiya remained." The old lady, fed up and angry, put a curse on the village, Auntie said, and the next day the hippies started dying. The ones who didn't left by the end of the week.

"What's this got to do with Kashmir?" Larry asked. He took a step forward, reducing the space between them.

She could explain it all away. She could just wish him luck. She could tell him she understood, he was different. Instead, she said, "Be careful."

When she left him, his mouth was tight like it had been the day she nearly hit him with the car. She wondered if he knew that the power of a curse came from the belief people put into it. She knew he would not ask himself why her aunties, who were afraid their niece had grown up irretrievably American, told these stories. For Larry, Meena finally understood, the power of an exotic curse made more sense than the desperation of flesh-and-blood people driven to terrorism. He'd been everywhere, seen everything, and in the end, he saw nothing at all.

When Meena stepped outside after her shift, the sun was rising, casting a weak light over the snow-covered cars. For the first time in weeks, her body didn't ache; she felt a tight flag inside come unfurled, and when the cold touched her fingers and face, it was a caress. She fell backward into the deepest patch of fresh snow she could find and made an angel, the first of the season. As she drove home in her wet clothes, she thought about the young boy who wanted to fly and wondered if he'd ever make it to Disney World. Would it live up to his expectations or would he emerge from childhood one day, not with the pre-fab memory of Mickey and Minnie, but a clear picture of a shallow cardboard box and himself suspended in mid-air, an angel in flight, between the table and the sofa.

The events remained filed in a place she could not reach. They surfaced years later when she read that Larry had died on a mountain climbing expedition, leading a group of amateurs up a peak in the Himalayas. She tried to imagine him in Kathmandu, and then in the small villages at the base of the mountain. She saw him, tall and fair, carrying himself like the Olympic torch among the throngs in the bazaar, the small brown bodies of boys and girls dancing around him, crying "Sahib, sahib, 25 paise only." He would joke with them and shoo them away like flies. But they didn't really annoy him. After a week, their low persistent voices had become a familiar tune. They understood each other, the beggars and Larry. Their presence was comforting. They were exactly what he'd expected, in synch with the stinking gullies and jasmine-scented temples around him. He saw the boys as they were and where they should be.

Up at base camp, Meena heard the tents flapping and smelled the hot, sweet chai the Sherpas would have made for the climbers. She tried to imagine the oxygen-light air at that altitude and felt only the embrace of frigid cold, a vise around her ribs and diaphragm as Larry tried to find the energy and breath to climb back down from the peak he'd scaled so many times in his dreams.

She wondered how he felt, dying a foreigner's death, alone in the snow and ice. His last sight before losing consciousness would have been the concerned faces of the Sherpas hovering over his glazed eyes and parched lips. These were faces that cared whether he lived or died. These faces he would have turned away from if he had seen them on the street in a small town in Western Massachusetts.

Meena snuggled deep under the rezai, the thick cotton quilt, a wedding gift from one of the aunties. She turned the pages of the glossy magazine carefully to avoid waking the sleeping body beside her. She'd finished her residency, and met the right man on her own, the one who had been raised in Texas and was still learning to love the cold. His details were humble, ordinary parents who, like hers, had chased the tropics in their new home. They went out a few times, and in the restaurant, she couldn't help noticing the way his eyes flicked from side to side as people walked by. He stared at women, women who didn't look like her, but when he fixed his brown eyes on Meena, she knew he saw her. He saw hair, body, and skin. He saw himself and did not look away.

He was a man who didn't need her to explain the way she'd looked at Larry, the dumb childhood jokes about Tonto and Chief Sitting Bull, or the precarious line she walked between native and foreigner. When she took him skating, he leaned on her briefly and then crossed one foot over the other and skated away, arms stretched out in a wide embrace of the pine and the blue-tipped fir around the frozen pond as his skates wobbled beneath him. Later, he practiced near the edge of the pond, knees bent awkwardly, eyes down so he could watch his feet move.

When Meena looked at the photo of Larry on the slick page that stuck to her fingers, she saw him as he'd always been: frozen and distant, cold to the touch. She closed the magazine and dropped it to the floor, next to her old, worn-out slippers. She thought she should feel something about his death, but she didn't. She thought she should feel sorry about this, but she felt nothing other than mild interest. They were strangers, after all. Anita had been right.

# Waterville

The virus spread through the city that summer like a rumor, invisible and difficult to pin down. Entire neighborhoods quarantined, summer camps and daycare centers shut down. People were on the move. City blocks emptied overnight, even as politicians and conspiracy theorists alike called for reason and calm.

Maria's arms and legs ached, and her lips were dry. She'd come home late from the restaurant and slept deeply, late into the morning. The citywide panic had put such a demand on the trucks that by the time she got to the U-Haul all she could get was a 6-footer. It was smaller than what she'd asked for, but she doubted there would be time to get everything her mother owned into the truck and still meet the noon deadline. She had asked her brother Jamie to go earlier in the month, but he was too busy at the hospital, acting like a doctor on a television drama, and so the job of moving her mother out of her quarantined neighborhood had fallen to Maria.

The demolition was scheduled to start today. At noon. Which gave Maria precisely two hours to get her mother's stuff into the truck and move her to the other side of the river. The riverbed had been dry for twenty years, yet everyone still called it the river, as if all they needed was one really big rain to fill it again. In this way, Waterville remained a hopeful city. Soon enough, it would be a river again. To Maria, though, it would always be the chasm, the gap between the house of her childhood and her adult apartment, high up above the city with its view of the dry desert lots and dying vegetation.

The truck in front of Maria moved slowly up the hill, leaving behind huge puffs of dust. There was no way around him, and the more Maria honked, the slower the driver seemed to go. She hoped her mother was packed and would be ready to go. She knew they wouldn't be able to take everything. Her mother's new one-bedroom apartment, two blocks from Maria's building, wouldn't be able to contain forty years' accumulation of fabric, yarn, embroidery kits, mason jars filled with buttons, not to mention the collection of salt and pepper shakers. She would have to leave it all behind, and this in itself was a blessing.

"You have to help her sort through all her crap," Jamie said on the phone. "Otherwise, she'll be miserable later."

"Hey," Maria snapped. "I have a job too."

But she knew serving food to rich people did not, for Jamie, count as a job. He was saving lives; she was merely maintaining them.

"And make sure she takes her meds," he said, before hanging up.

The truck turned off Lindbergh Street, leaving Maria in a cloud of dust and black smoke. If she hadn't been coughing, she might have wondered where it was going; instead, she cursed and looked for her water, then cursed some more when she found the bottle was dry. She knew the real reason they were kicking her mother and her neighbors out—water. It was a hideously expensive and destructive plan to divert a river up north and flood the ravine, bringing water back to the sadly named Waterville. How the river dried up in the first place was attributed to sudden climate change, though Maria's mother had recently told her that the water had been secretly diverted to fuel development. What development and where, her mother couldn't say. Maria put her conspiracy theory down to her resistance to moving. Meanwhile, the city was snapping up properties on this side of the ravine with no apology. Eminent domain required none. This was the first neighborhood to be evacuated, but it would not be the last.

"Mom?" Maria called as the screen door slammed behind her.

No answer. And as her eyes adjusted from the bright sunshine to the dimness of the small house, she realized she was standing in the one clear space in the whole living room. It looked as if her mother had emptied every single closet, seized by a sudden emotion she could not control. There wasn't a single place to sit—clothes piled high on the sofa and chairs, books in piles on the floor, a wicker stool on the coffee table, a ceramic fish lying on its side next to a stack of old newspaper.

Maria's head throbbed. She needed water and an aspirin. In the kitchen, she found some cranberry juice in the dark refrigerator, took her aspirin, and cursed the municipal, county, and city governments, adding the governor, the President, and Homeland Security for good measure. She looked out of the window above the sink. The backyard pitched away from the house, towards the ravine. Her parents had installed a fence at the end of their lot to keep the kids from wandering into the growth of sumac and bamboo, but Jamie had found a weakness in the fence and had tunneled through as far as he could go. He was good at that—finding weaknesses, picking at them until the structure gave.

Something moved by the ironwood tree. It was her mother, still wearing her pajamas, a ratty old white shirt and loose blue pants that Jamie had tried to replace with something silky. It was a pointless gift; like Maria, their mother dressed only to please herself. Their mother may have been most proud of Jamie, but it was Maria who understood her best. At least, this was what Maria liked to think.

When she heard the back door slam, Maria's mother got up from her knees, leaning heavily on the tree for support. All the years of yoga, juice fasts, and detox baths, and still she'd gotten old. At seventy, she moved with effort. When had she become old? To Maria, she was still mother—exasperating, embarrassing, a good cook and a bad driver who lost her reading glasses every other day, something she had been doing for as long as Maria could remember. And yet she was competent in her way. She finished every project she started—quilts, curtains, hand-knitted hats and socks she gave as gifts. So why couldn't she finish packing?

"Max is gone," her mother said across the yard. She was holding some knitting needles and yarn, as if she were about to start a new project. She liked to start new projects before she went on a trip. How many times had she stayed up all night before leaving home, not packing, but going through her stash in search of the perfect traveling project?

"Where?"

"He didn't leave a note," her mother snapped. "I opened the front door, and he just took off. I think he knows something's up. Dogs are sensitive that way."

"You find him," Maria said. "I have to pack."

She stomped back into the house, grabbed some black garbage bags and started filling them—clothes, books and paper. In the distance, she heard the back up beep of a truck, a pause, and then boom—the sound of a house coming down. At least, that's what she assumed it was, and this now explained the truck that had blocked her way, then turned on Lindbergh, which would have led it straight to the Macgregors' place, the last one at the end of the cul-de-sac. The Macgregors had had five kids crammed into their three-bedroom house, and they'd been gone for a week already, happy to take their money and move to another city, one with a decent water supply and land to call their own.

When Maria went back to check on her mother, she saw that Max had returned, and her mother was sitting against the ironwood tree, with the dog in her lap, shoving something down his throat. Maria wasn't sure what made Max so dumb— the seizures, the high dose of pheno, or the fact that he was a yellow lab, over bred and overfed, incapable of anything but affection.

As she approached them, dog and mother, she saw that her mother was sitting at an awkward angle, almost flush against the tree, as if she had lost the use of her legs. Max squirmed in her lap.

"He's too old for that," Maria said. "Give him to me."

"We're not leaving," her mother said.

"Too late."

"You said you'd call the county. You said you'd get a lawyer to look into it. You promised."

There was no denying the hurt in her mother's voice.

"Well, Jamie—"

"Jamie is on call every day. The ER is understaffed. This virus going around—it has them running all day. He's busy, Maria, which is why I asked you."

Her mother's face was flushed, and Maria realized the mess in the living room was rage. Only it wasn't directed at the city.

"Did you take your pills?" Jamie had been very specific. "If she ends up in the ER," he'd said, "It's on you."

"I'm not going anywhere."

Maria left the house. She needed to walk, clear her head, which was in the dull ache stage of her hangover. What exactly happened last night? She vaguely remembered the flames of a Baked Alaska, a steak sent back twice, a hair floating on the surface of tomato soup, shots of tequila handed to her as she ran back and forth between kitchen and dining room. Had the chef convinced her to streak around the dried up fountain at the park? She had a lot of naked stories, unfortunately. That was the problem. At least she'd woken up in her underwear, in her own bed.

She ended up at the Macgregors' place. It was only half demolished, and a couple of men in hard hats were milling around, looking confused. Then they got into a car and drove away, leaving behind a Mexican or Indian man standing next to the semi-rubble of the house. He was slight, with dark wavy hair and a round face. He was checking something off on a plastic clipboard with the name of a pharmaceutical company on it.

"They were supposed to let us salvage the wood, windows and built-ins. These old houses have amazing hinges."

"Hinges?"

"And great glass doorknobs. I sent the demolition crew away to talk to their boss. It was all agreed." He pulled out his cell phone and stared at it.

"You can't get service here," Maria said. "But I have a house for you. You can have the stained glass, the cabinets, the spindles. Whatever."

His face lit up, his teeth white and shiny against his smooth brown skin. "Cool," he said.

He introduced himself, "Ravi, named after a river in India," and followed Maria back to the house. If the mess in the living room surprised him, he didn't give it away. His face remained placid and still, his round brown eyes unreadable as he took it all in, the stained glass windows on either side of the bookcase, the mantle with it's carvings that Maria used to trace as a child. Her mother had told her there was a magic kingdom up the chimney and if she were good and sat quietly, one day it would reveal itself to her.

"First," Maria said, "you have to help me pack and load all this stuff into the U-Haul. Leave the curtains, the fabric, and the yarn. Anything that isn't in a plastic box stays. Then the house is yours."

"No problem," and he took three bags out to the truck.

Maria went out back with her mother's pills and a glass of cranberry juice. Her mother was still under the tree. The dog was gone. Her mother was knitting a sock. Maria recognized the four double-pointed needles, the ribbing at the top of a cuff. The yarn was thick, and Maria wondered who the intended recipient was—her or Jamie.

"You know, it's bad luck to turn a heel twice," her mother said. She was about four inches into the cuff, and it was clear to Maria that she had made no effort to keep the dog with her.

"Where's Max?"

Her mother jerked her head towards the hole in the fence.

Maria sighed. She held out the glass and the pills, and then noticed that her mother was chained to the tree. Not with rope, or yarn, or a bit of fabric tied together, but a real chain, the kind she would have had to purchase at a hardware store, locked in not one, but three places. Three different combination locks. How had she done it, Maria wondered. Had Max suddenly developed opposable thumbs?

Maria willed herself to put the glass and the pills down on the base of the concrete sundial. She twirled one of the locks. For years, her mother's favorite combination had been 000. She couldn't remember anything else. But now the locks stayed locked, and the chain stayed wrapped. Maria wondered if Ravi had a bolt cutter in his car.

"I'm not leaving until Max comes back." Her mother's hands moved quickly, the nickel-plated needles flashing like streaks of lightning.

When had her mother, this nice old lady with white hair and soft brown eyes who had tried so hard to hide her disappointment in her daughter, become the kind of woman who could go to Home Depot, ask for the right kind of chain, memorize three different combinations? She knew Maria too well—the unfinished dissertation, incomplete relationships, and half-baked life—and she knew that despite the promise, it would be another month before Maria showed up again. The riverbed was narrow, but the distance between them was great, and Maria had never felt it more than at this moment.

"If I find Max, will you tell me the combination?"

Her mother nodded. She was counting stitches, only half listening.

"Promise?"

"He's always loved you best."

Maria went back inside. Ravi was packing the salt and pepper shaker collection, wrapping each one in newspaper, placing them carefully in a box.

"Those are hers," Maria said, suddenly feeling possessive.

"No problem," Ravi said. He was on the Easter sets: pastel eggs, yellow chicks with tiny holes in the top of their heads, snow white bunnies with holes in their pink noses.

"Don't you feel bad, dismantling other people's houses? Like hyenas or vultures."

Ravi smiled and continued wrapping the salt and pepper Chrysler building. "That's my partner, Paul. He'll stay away until the last minute. I'll evaluate the houses today, so he'll come back and help me strip them before demolition starts next week."

"Next week? Not today?"

Ravi nodded. "We have a contract with the city. That crew was early."

For the first time that day, Maria felt light. She would call the lawyer and leave a message on his machine today. Then she would sort through her mother's things, pack them carefully. They could even take the extra yarn and fabric, given the extra time. If her mother thought they could save the house, she'd leave willingly. But not without Max. Maria had to find him first.

When Maria went out back, Max was lying on the grass, next to her mother, eyes closing as he settled in for a nap.

"Where did he come from?"

Her mother did not look up. "Twenty-eight, twenty-nine.... thirty-two." She looped the yarn over her forefinger. "Through that hole you made."

"For the last time, I did not make that hole. Jamie did. He's the one who always wanted to leave home. He's the one who thought life would be better on the other side. He's the one who left and didn't look back." Maria's hands were clenched, her voice hoarse with frustration. Christ, she needed a beer. Or something.

"It's true," her mother said. "You never wanted to leave home. If things could have stayed the same forever, you would have been happy."

But she was really talking about herself. Maria finally understood: the late nights of knitting instead of packing; the "just one more row" before she'd put on her shoes and coat; the frantic search for the missing needle or specific project—all delaying tactics. A new project was not about launching a trip. It was about postponing one. Just like a new research topic or another book to read or a new development in the field had postponed the end of Maria's dissertation, so each new project kept her mother home. The piles of fabric, the baskets of yarn, the new dishcloths and curtains every six months lined the house like feathers in a nest.

In a week, the whole neighborhood would be gone. No matter how many lawyers Maria called, she understood the law of eminent domain, the necessity of destruction for the public good. The houses, blue, green and white bungalows once made a pretty picture with kids running in and out all day, lawns littered with toys, barking dogs, and the constant smell of barbecue. Now there was silence and the place smelled antiseptic. The carefully tended gardens—roses, lilac, and bougainvillea—looked plastic.

If only the river had not dried up.

"Give me the combination," Maria said, kneeling down by her mother. "Let me help you."

Her mother kept on knitting. She did not look up.

# Border Crossing

1.  Maybe you're wondering, if the cardinal is Ohio's state bird, why the St. Louis Cardinals? Or the Arizona Cardinals? I don't give a shit about baseball or football, but I still want to impress you. I'm thinking of 95 clever and interesting topics for discussion. The worth of a signed Longaberger basket, the way two rivers become three in Pittsburgh, the origins of the perogie pizza. On a two-lane highway yesterday, I followed a New Hampshire license plate: Live Free or Die. A woman driving in the other lane swore as she passed me, her face scrunched up in anger. Yes, my driving still sucks. Yes, I'm still mad at you. No, I'm not coming home.

Seven states claim the cardinal as their bird.

I found this postcard at a diner near Tappan Lake.

I will always love you, Jon. But I don't understand you.

2.  One minute I was driving to Columbus, the next I was in Mackinaw City, having followed an Ontario plate: Yours to Discover. Or Plunder, as you used to say. You never really forgave us for winning the 1812 War. I couldn't stop myself from driving over the bridge; I fall in love with the water glittering like a million fish scales in the sun. I don't have my passport, but I told the border guard at Sault Ste. Marie I was visiting my aging mother-in-law whose son was too busy with his Academic Career and had not visited in two years. Then I told her what you did, and she agreed that a little time away might do us some good. I gave her my driver's license, and she asked if I was carrying a gun.

No gun, no alcohol, no fruit. Just a grudge and a bar of chocolate.

She smiled. Even the border guard gets me.

I did not tell her I have no intention of going home.

3.  Your mother says hi. When I showed up in Elliot Lake yesterday, she buzzed me in as if she'd been expecting me. She acts like it's completely normal for her daughter-in-law to show up without her son. Perhaps you're wondering what we talk about. She knows you're a jerk, I can tell by the questions she doesn't ask. Instead, we talk about easy things: the yard sale we'll attend tomorrow, the bear who wandered into town last week and cleaned out the dumpster at Canadian Legion. I helped her serve lunch there today, and one of the old guys came up to me and said, "That Sadie. She's still got it going on."

Your mother has not asked why we haven't visited—she doesn't want to hear about the Great Tenure Track, that railroad of infinite destination with multiple stops along the way: associate, full, distinguished, very distinguished. She's proud of you all right, she just isn't sure why. Conference papers delivered in Taiwan are no substitute for flesh-and-blood grandchildren.

I have not asked about the blueberries growing on the old tailings behind the uranium mine. She gave them to me on frozen cheesecake last night, and I enjoyed the thought of radioactive anti-oxidants traveling through my body. A reverse detox. The perfect metaphor for our relationship.

4.　When my parents died, I resolved to be kind to old people. This is why, instead of telling your mother I hate scented soaps—as you or your sister might—I tried to flush the blueberry-scented elephant down the toilet. When it didn't go down, I fished it out and wrapped it in a bunch of grocery bags and put it in the trash. While your mother was at her darts tournament today, I threw out a bag of sour milk, two boxes of stale cereal, and a piece of furry blue cheese. I saved the potatoes she had boiled to show her how black they were under their skins. She claimed she just bought them and I did not argue, just put them in the trash.

You might try being human once in a while. When you're out with your wife, at a fancy faculty party, you might smile at her across the room while Professor Very Distinguished bores her with his research on medieval artifacts found in Shake-speare. Or instead of correcting the way she uses her fork, you might pour her a glass of wine, brush the back of your hand against her cheek. Better yet, try not to wince when she mispronounces "synecdoche." While you were in a classroom talking about the importance of metaphor, she was working in an office, the real world where a cardinal is just a cardinal.

Your mother's smile takes up her whole face. The best thing she ever did was to ignore your dad's advice to have all her teeth pulled and replaced with dentures.

5. Perhaps it's childish to leave your husband of ten years after you catch him reading your journal like it's *People* magazine at the gym, just waiting for any-sweaty-body to pick it up. After all, your mother did not leave your father when he and your grandfather had that big fight while playing cards, and she beat them with a slipper to get them to stop. She did not leave your father when he came home drunk and told her she was slovenly. She did not leave him when he accused her of cheating at Scrabble.

Ten years gone, and this is where we are: I'm still trying to impress you, and you're still trying to figure me out. Maybe there isn't much of a difference other than a PhD between you and your father. He crossed lines as if they didn't exist, and if your mother had kept a journal, he'd have read it with no apology. If you still don't understand what the big deal is—what it means to a person to have her secret hopes and dreams and mistakes exposed to a committee of one like some academic dissertation, which my journals most certainly are not—well, you have truly crossed over to the dark side.

And I bet they didn't even ask for your passport.

# Her Mother's Ashes

She hears the children at the front door before she sees them. They rush into the hall, a mass of slickers and rubber rain boots, squeaking and slipping across the floor. Lally remembers when raincoats came only in yellow, and suddenly, she feels old. From the room, Lally watches them tear their coats off, struggle with their outdoor shoes, grabbing onto each other or the wall for support, laughing and breathless. Joke trips into the classroom, still wearing her red galoshes.

When she started working at the afterschool program, Lally told the children that while growing up, she wasn't allowed to wear shoes in the house. The one exception was the time her parents went to Boston and brought back a pair of red Oxfords for her. They were new and clean, shiny and beautiful; she'd worn them to bed that night. Her parents didn't know they were called Oxfords; for years the shoes were simply Boston shoes, the only shoes she ever wore indoors.

"Joke," Lally calls out, anxious to get her before she takes another step into the clean classroom.

Joke looks up.

"Don't you want to put on your slippers?" Lally asks. The children take their shoes off when they come in and put on the slippers lined up under their pegs in the hallway. She doesn't want to tell Joke what to do, but the order is implicit in her question, said in a tone used only with children.

Joke looks down at her feet, as if surprised to see her outdoor shoes still there.

Before Lally knows it, they are standing around her, their strange little voices trying to drown each other out. Some of them have surprisingly low voices, as if they've been staying up late nights with a bottle of whiskey and a pack of cigarettes. They are short enough to trip her without trying. Looking down at them, she feels very tall and awkward, not old but young now, like an unsure teenager.

"Tell us about the thousand-ton man, again, please Lally, please?"

"Twelve-hundred-pound-man," she says automatically, and then wonders what difference accuracy makes to a story culled from the *National Enquirer* and the evening news.

"Whatever. Tell me what he eats."

"I told you yesterday, Davey."

Davey is giggling behind his hands. He loves this story, as do his ten giggling cohorts, standing in a rough semi-circle at her feet.

"Okay." She sighs. Why do children love to hear the same story again and again? "But only if you promise, all of you, not to get on my nerves."

They nod, sort of, and shuffle to the big low table in the middle of the room. Over the sound of chairs scraping the floor, a question:

"What's get on your nerves?"

As the afternoon progresses to dusk, they draw pictures of the twelve-hundred-pound man. His profile, his bedroom, his chins, his tummies. The man stuck in the bathroom doorway. What he eats for breakfast, what he will look like after his diet, what he eats on his diet. They draw his life inside out, and when she tries to show them a photo of the real fat man, they are dismissive, as if his existence could never measure up to their stories.

She has never considered herself a storyteller, a necessary skill for this job that fits her like her old school coat—several sizes too big, with the saleslady's assurance she'd grow into it. At first, she felt herself shrinking. When the children crowded around her feet, she'd pull into herself, like a flower closing up for the night. Eventually she reached a comfort zone where she no longer felt the automatic closing off. Now, however, when she tells the same story again and again, she moves neither forward nor back.

Lally tries to read while they draw, but they won't let her. All the attention goes to the fat man. The questions and comments are constant. Lally gives up on her book, drawn into their world in spite of herself. It amazes her how fresh their fascination is, how their incredulity grows each day. They greet the story like a long-favorite fairy tale.

Lally's mother didn't tell fairy tales. Instead, she would tell her about the Partition. "We lost everything. We had so much, and then, one day, we had nothing but the clothes we wore." Independence Day did not mean freedom; it meant Partition, the day Lahore became part of Pakistan forever.

Lally wanted to hear more, but even at ten she knew that if she asked for a happy ending, her mother would clamp her lips tight and walk away. Instead, she imagines her mother, eighteen and frightened, holding onto her uncle's hand—the little boy her grandfather so desperately waited for, through five daughters and two miscarriages—as they board a train bound for Hoshiarpur. What would it feel like to travel without luggage? Now when Lally's mother traveled, she packed large, unwieldy suitcases, stuffing packs of dry cereal and powdered milk into the corners as if she would never see food again.

"Your great-grandfather was the richest man in Lahore. He had a big house—the joint family lived there—and he had his own shop. One day he saw two young men eyeing my fifteen-year-old cousin. He had two of his men kill them the next day."

"Didn't anyone say or do anything?" Lally was stalling, hoping to distract her mother, so that she would not have time before school to finish off the cold, milky dregs of oatmeal in her bowl.

"Nope." Her mother covered her toast in marmalade, thick and sickly sweet. The morning paper was spread over her half of the kitchen table, and she read while crunching her toast, occasionally brushing the crumbs from the page.

"Why not?"

Her mother shrugged, turning the page. "That's the way it was. It's the parents' duty to take care of the girls, to protect them and make sure they are settled."

Even then, Lally knew what "settled" meant. It meant a home. It meant a doctor or engineer husband, a house in Cherry Hill, and two children—a boy, first, for the family, and then a girl, for herself.

"Did that girl, your cousin, ever get married?"

Her mother sighed, and her lips tightened. She looked up from her paper. "She ran off with a Muslim boy, a few years before the partition. Grandfather was so stupid; he thought everything would stay the same, that nothing would change. He let the girl go, and we never saw her again."

"Why not? Where did she go?"

Her mother started clearing the dishes from the table, her toast half-eaten, Lally's oatmeal forgotten. "You're going to be late for school. Come on, now. You're making me late."

Later, on the corner of Elm Street, the point where Lally would walk to school by herself, her mother said, as if there had never been a pause, "We used to see that girl in the market sometimes. I wanted to speak to her, but grandmother wouldn't let me. By the time I found out where she lived, it was too late. It was 1947. We went on holiday, and never came back."

She hugged herself against the chilly autumn air, crunching dry leaves under her feet. When Lally turned back to wave, from half way down the block, she was gone, already around the corner.

When Lally's mother died a year ago, Lally was in India, waiting for her. In between her tears, Lally smiled at the irony of her mother dying in New York, visiting friends for a few days before her flight to Delhi, when her express wish had been to have her ashes scattered in the Ganges. Lally dutifully obliged her mother, making the round trip, hassling with customs officials who gave in only when she started to cry, trekking up to the Ganges for the first time in her life, and finally, mingling with pilgrims and hippies on the banks, surreptitiously slipping her mother's ashes into the water. Looking around self-consciously, she noticed a couple of men bathing upriver, while a man in white beat some clothes against the rocks. At first she was repulsed by the brown water with islands of foam and flecks of ash floating on its surface. A line of marigolds, rose petals, and lighted clay lamps bobbed past her. The smell from the nearby ghats bothered her—it felt like she was breathing the dust of the dead—but she had learned that actively resisting a smell only made it worse.

A long time ago, when she was nine, Lally watched her mother feed her father's ashes into the Connecticut River with equal surreptitiousness. He'd always been slightly perturbed by her mother's wish to be scattered in the Ganges—"This is your home now," he'd say, pointing to the Berkshires that encircled the small Massachusetts town he taught in. But that had been no more her mother's home than this was.

Lally looked around to see if anyone else was doing the same thing—she didn't know the proper ritual, the right prayers. She'd been too embarrassed to ask her aunt; the family already thought she hadn't been raised properly. All she had were her mother's stories. What did they mean? Lally hears her mother's voice. "Saraswati sits on your tongue once a day; she is the goddess who watches us for correct speech. When I was ten, I said, 'One day we're going to lose all of this.' We lost everything. No home, no business, no nothing. My parents had to start all over again." And that was it. She never said how she felt, and the harder Lally tried to remember, the less she knew.

Dusk fell, and Lally stood on the banks of the muddy river, waiting for someone to tell her what to do. The cawing of the crows grated her ears, and she hesitantly opened the urn. But as she became absorbed in her task, less concerned with everything around her, more concerned with the ashes, with saying goodbye to her mother, who she would never see again, who would probably not even be able to come back as a ghost now that she was ash, Lally slowly left her perch on the sandstone bank and waded into the water. When all the ashes were gone, and she was left with an empty urn, she realized she was crying.

Lally missed part of the fourteen-day grieving period, wanting to dispose of the ashes immediately, almost afraid she'd forget her mother's directive. Family and friends crowded into the living room, the women seated on the Persian carpet, dominating the conversation, the men on the periphery of the over-decorated room, uncomfortably perched on the over-stuffed couch. The room was dark, even during the day, built deliberately to avoid the hot summer sun. Lally's grandfather built this house after the partition, working two jobs to resettle his family. The house took two years to build, and by then Lally's mother had already left for the States.

Lally couldn't stay in New Delhi, with the family, because they reminded her too much of her mother. The way her two aunts cackled in Punjabi, the heavy, spicy smell of the food, the lingering scent of jasmine soap on her cousins' skin—it was familiar and unknown, both at the same time.

At the end of her last meal in New Delhi, she asked her youngest aunt about the missing cousin, the one who ran off with the Muslim. "I wouldn't know," her aunt said, getting up to clear the table. "Such things weren't discussed in my presence."

By the next day, the fat man is old news. The children are bored with his story, have exhausted it in their discussions and play. Lally tries to read to them from a book of fairy tales donated by one of the parents.

She is barely into the first paragraph, when Joke announces, "This story sucks. My mom's always trying to tell it to me."

"Yeah, it's stupid. No one reads it anymore," Davey says.

The other children agree, in varying levels of disgust. Lally watches the class dissolve.

"Hey, Lally?" Davey shouts above the growing chaos.

"What?" She stands up, hoping to restore her authority.

"Tell us another story like the fat man."

"I can't."

The fat man seems inspired now, as if it came from nowhere. She has no idea why they liked him so much. She tries to think, to remember when she last read anything of interest.

"I don't know any more stories like the fat man."

Joke picks her nose. "Make one up."

"Only if you take your finger out of your nose." She's been trying to break Joke and Missy of the habit, at least in public. "And the rest of you, sit down and be quiet for a few minutes so I can think."

The chairs scrape. After a few seconds, Davey raises his hand.

"Can I have some O's? I'm hungry."

Suddenly, everyone is hungry. She passes out bowls of sugarless Cheerios. Lally would give them cookies, but this is the only food the parents could agree on as a healthy snack.

"Okay. No interruptions, otherwise there won't be a story. You can draw if you want, but no talking while I talk, okay?"

Michael, the peewee of the bunch, settles his head down on the table. Joke does the same. Missy is sucking her thumb and Davey sits up straight, ready to draw.

"Well, my mother came from a huge family. Her mother was only sixteen when she was born and, somehow, in all the confusion, the family forgot when my mother was born. She never knew when her birthday really was, February 8, 14, or 28. All she knew for sure was the year and the place." What she doesn't say, what she can't say, is the disappointment of a first-born girl child was so keen, that her grandfather first asked the doctor if he was certain and then told him that maybe he should check again. It wasn't until her third birthday that it occurred to him to record the date of birth. Lally's grandmother used to tell this story, while bragging about her gone-to-America daughter, laughing at her dead husband's foolishness.

"Does that mean she had three birthdays?" Missy looks upset.

"Yup." For a long time, Lally gave her mother three birthday presents, as if to make up for her grandfather's neglect.

"Cool," Davey looks up from his O's.

"One day, when my mother was four years old, her grandmother, who was my great-grandmother, took her to her cousin's wedding in the next town. Her mother was too sick to go, but she didn't mind going with her grandmother." Too late, Lally pauses, trying to invoke her mother's voice, the way the story was told.

"In those days, a wedding was a pretty big deal. My mother got a new pair of shoes and a new dress. All her other relatives were going and since they had to go early, it was arranged that great-grandmother would pick my mother up at five o'clock that day."

Everyone is looking at Lally, except Joke, who is asleep. She can hear them breathing, watching her, waiting. It's raining outside and the sound of the cars whooshing up the street is familiar and comforting.

"Back then, not many people had their own cars. The wedding guests decided to catch an early bus to the town, since it would take three hours to get there. When great-grandmother picked my mother up, she was dressed in her new outfit, with new ribbons in her hair."

"Was she wearing her new shoes?"

"Yes."

"What kind of shoes?" Davey wants to know.

"Red Boston shoes," Lally improvises, using a vague yet definite term. It is difficult for her to see the shoes, the dress, her mother younger than she ever knew her.

To her surprise, he nods, as if he knows exactly what she's talking about. Everyone has had a pair of special shoes at one time or another.

Lally continues the story. "On the bus, there were just tons of people, mostly relatives, but also some neighbors and friends, who happened to be on the same bus. Great-grand-mother put my mother in a window seat, so she could watch the sun rise. When the bus started, she went off to the back to talk to the family.

"The last thing my mother remembers is the sun didn't rise quickly enough. The sky was purple and she could still see stars. She fell asleep."

Joke is awake now, her eyes wide and pinned to Lally. Davey is drawing a bus. He stops and looks up.

"Then what?" he says.

"Then the bus broke down in the middle of the road. A flat tire. So everyone got out to watch the driver change the tire. Then they got back on and were on their way. Somehow, my mother slept through it all.

"Well, they're finally pulling into town and great-grand-mother returns to her seat to find my mother. But she's not there anymore. Great-grandmother figures one of the aunts took her but when she gets off the bus no one has her. Natu-rally, she's upset. Someone starts yelling at the driver, saying it's all his fault. One aunt is praying, several others are crying. Great-grandmother gets back on the bus with her nephew, Biku. The bus is completely empty and they find my mother curled up sound asleep under a seat. Her new shoes are gone. When great-grandmother asks her what happened, she can't remember; she was too fast asleep."

"And then?"

"And then they went to the wedding and had a great time."

"But what about her shoes?" Missy pulls her thumb out. Every time Lally tells her not to suck it, she cries.

"Well, the shoes were gone."

"But what did she do? Did she get a new pair? Where were they?" All questions Lally had asked, all unanswered. Either she was making her mother late for work or trying to avoid doing homework—her mother, who had never heard of dodge ball, became an expert without even trying.

Several children look up. Davey is scribbling hard. Lally doesn't think he can help her this time.

"Well, she couldn't do anything. Someone had obviously taken them."

Lally remembers her mother telling the story as an example of how spoiled and loved she was by the elders in her family. She used to say that she'd lost the shoes.

"Who? Who took your mother's shoes?"

"Yeah, and how old was she again?"

"She was four years old and they never found the person who took her shoes. She was asleep when it happened."

"Did she cry?" Missy has to know.

"No. She never cried."

No, her mother never cried, not when she lost her shoes, not when she lost everything. Lally wants to ask her: did she lose her home or was it taken? Her mother tried so hard to tell only the good, as if Saraswati had taken permanent residence on her tongue, yet always, "We lost everything," reverberated under her words. Lally wants to answer their questions, to give them a happy ending, but she can't.

The fat man wanted to lose weight, to live an easy, unencumbered life. Lally knows only that her mother wanted a home. She hears her mother's single request: "Cremate me and throw my ashes in the Ganges. She is my home now."

"Poor little baby," Michael says to Joke, shaking his head.

"Didn't anybody love her?" Davey wants to know.

Lally sees Missy's face falling, in seconds, the droopy mouth, jutting lower lip, teary eyes. She cannot think of anything to say to make it better. This is the way her mother told the story, no more and no less. Lally can't imagine it told differently.

• • •

Lally turns on the evening news and wanders around the apartment. Photographs of her and her parents are scattered haphazardly between photos of friends and old faded photos of her mother's family, somehow rescued from falling into that gap that split India and Pakistan. When her grandfather died, his family put up a color portrait above the dining table and hung fresh garlands of jasmine and marigolds from it. When Lally was at the house in New Delhi, she wondered how they could stand the pain of seeing him while they ate. Her aunt remarked, when she saw Lally staring, "It is the children's duty to love and honor the parents. If we don't, then our children will forget us."

Lally comes out of her bedroom in time to hear a news item about the fat man, who has died from a heart attack. His heart couldn't take the fluctuations in weight and now his family is suing the doctor who put him on a diet. "If only we'd accepted his weight," the mother is saying, "he'd still be alive. We thought we were doing the right thing. All we wanted was for him to be happy."

Lally hopes that none of the children find out.

It's raining the next morning when Lally wakes up. When she gets to school in the early afternoon, her mind is unfocused, scattered over the many things she should and must do beyond the walls of the classroom. She remembers that this is a temporary job, that she is unsettled and on her way elsewhere.

A block from school, she breaks the rules and buys the children a pack of chocolate chip cookies. One won't hurt them.

The children come in helter-skelter, more restless than usual. They have been indoors too much lately. If it weren't raining, Lally would take them to the park by the river, near Sutton Place, although she always worries about a lawsuit brought on by a broken arm and her irresponsibility.

They gather around the table, where Lally has set up some modeling clay. Missy is the last to come in, still wearing her rain boots and clutching her bunny slippers close.

"Hey Missy," Lally says, "You forgot to take your boots off. Come here, I'll help you with them." She nearly adds, "Silly goose," but something stops her.

"No. I have to keep them on."

Lally briefly wonders if this is an edict from Mr. Kaputsy. "Well, then why don't we put your slippers back?"

"No. I want to keep them with me," Missy whines.

The other children toy with their clay, listening, watching.

"Missy," Lally says, "you really shouldn't wear rain boots inside. They're dirty."

"No, they're not. The rain made them clean."

"Well, you need to let your feet breathe."

"No, I don't. I won't," she says loudly.

"Why?"

Missy is sniffing and gasping, about to cry.

"That's okay, Miss, keep your boots on. I just wanted to know why. You sit next to Davey, over here, okay?"

After much effort to get them settled with drawing paper and crayons as well as the clay that's already out, Davey breaks the tenuous silence, almost thinking out loud, his head still bent over his work.

"What happened to the fat man?"

"He's dead," Lally says, and instantly feels regret mingled with irritation. If Davey hadn't suddenly broken her daydreaming, she would not have been caught so unawares. She doesn't want to talk about the fat man or her mother anymore.

"Yeah," Davey nods, sagely. "That's what my mom said, but I didn't believe her."

The other children are listening, as if the fat man's fate does not surprise them. They whisper quietly amongst themselves, with few questions. It is easier for people to mourn those they know, or think they know. The fat man never fooled the children into believing he was anything more, and the children knew him as well as they could. They have no regrets now; there was never any more to know about him once they'd answered all their questions.

Lally understands that she has become that storyteller she thought she never was, but there is no comfort in this. Her mother's stories concealed more than they revealed, and the regret that has been gnawing at her all this time now washes over her like the muddy waters of the Ganges. She should feel cleansed, refreshed; instead, a wave of nausea hits her and she has to bite her lip to hold herself still. Lally gets up to give the children their cookies.

Her mother has found her home now, but where has she left her daughter? Lally can finally see a face on the four-year-old forgotten under the seat of a bus. It is her own.

# Home Is Another Country on TV

I saw their pictures in the paper, in the subway, on my way to work. I saw them, and I couldn't believe it, and I looked at them again. Then I just stared at them, at the gray-toned school photos, their faces blurred and grainy on the newsprint. I stared at them in the glaring lights of the subway car, as bodies pressed against me from either side and a briefcase banged my knee, not once, but twice, and if the owner apologized, I didn't hear him.

That night you call me and want to know why. Why two fourteen-year-old girls would lay themselves down in front of the LIRR, the commuter line for chrissakes, as if Amtrak or the subway would have made more sense, and greet their death holding hands? They were good girls, you say. You want to claim them, but you don't know them, not much better than the journalist who reports what she sees—successful parents, suburban homes, the best education money can buy, their smiling faces—and then tells the reader no one knows why they died.

Their hands were still together, afterwards, and you ask me why, as if I have the answer. I hear the desperation in your voice, and I wonder what exactly you don't understand, what it is you want me to remember, and why you think that will make you feel better. You were there too, you saw what I saw, and for ten years, we have not talked about it. And now the decision of two little girls with black hair, brown skin, and parents who speak a labored English, makes you pick up the phone and ask me for answers I do not have.

What I remember first is the look in Zed's eyes when we walked into that dark apartment, the wood floor already sticky with beer, the big muscular men crowding the galley kitchen, some of them still in muddy rugby clothes, others smelling of Old Spice or Brut, manly teenaged smells they would never outgrow. Zed's eyes turned to black pools of oil as he absorbed the scene, still and calm in the midst of raucous post-game heartiness.

"She didn't say it was a rugby party."

I shrugged. Zed was my friend. It had been his idea to come: he wanted to see Sarah. Had to see her. And since he was my friend, and I didn't want him to be left pasted against the wall, ignoring every other woman in the room just in case Sarah threw a smile at him, I tagged along.

We walked through the narrow hallway, past the bedrooms on either side, pushing through the inevitable cluster around the bathroom where the keg took up most of the space. Rob, who was English, stood by the door, explaining that Sarah didn't want beer slopping all over her floors. He had ragged brown hair, muscular legs that strained against his jeans, and a chipped front tooth. Flecks of gray bristle on his chin caught the light like glitter. Every woman who walked by stopped to talk to him.

"He gets away with it because of the accent," Zed muttered as he pumped beer. "Think if I had bad teeth and put on some off-the-boat, no-speaky-English accent, girls would talk to me?"

Zed's teeth were white, evenly spaced Chiclets that were almost unnatural in their perfection. Second-generation teeth, he called them, for his Chinese parents both had terrible teeth and were always taking him to the dentist.

I said nothing, and he scowled and handed me my beer.

"It smells like an airplane bathroom here," he said. "I'm going up to the roof."

I started to follow him, but a hand on my upper arm stopped me.

"Do I know you?"

I had met Rob before, at one of Sarah's other parties, where I first heard him tell the story about his chipped tooth. I can no longer remember the details of the story, only its existence. What I remember is stopping, letting Zed get ahead of me, and listening to Rob's story once again, never mentioning that I had heard it before. I was a little surprised he didn't remember me, the talisman Sarah acquired in college when she was sleeping with Jag Desai. For a while, I had been her advisor on all things Indian, though the only Indians I knew well were my parents and my sister. Jag was long gone (replaced by Tom, then you), but I remained because when you're young and living in Manhattan for the first time, you need all the friends you have. I was a remnant of Sarah's past, not quite her present, and definitely not her future.

That bitter understanding did not stop me from listening to Rob's story, letting him light my cigarette, and enjoying the feel of his callused fingertips on my hands as we cupped the lighter against some non-existent wind. I remember the pull, the way I lingered until a blonde in a tight tank top came along, and his green eyes left my face. I was dismissed.

These days we smile at each other across the room at a party, promise to meet for lunch, and then two months later, when I find your number tucked in my wallet, it's too late to call, and I've forgotten why we exchanged numbers in the first place. In college, we swore we'd be friends forever, but after we graduated, the only time Zed and I saw you was at the occasional party. Your job was demanding, you said, and you couldn't just hang out during the week. By the time I saw you at Sarah's, you'd become someone I used to know.

Sometimes I blame the beer, go over the number of times we went back to that bathroom, filled our cups and took them up to the roof. How else to account for what happened that night, and the nights that followed, when I would come home and stare at the phone, careful to keep the TV low, in case I missed the ring? And how would that help you, and your two girls, classmates, confidantes, comrades in arms?

Later, we were sitting on the roof, Zed and I, watching the television through the window in one of the apartments across the street. The blue light flickered in the dark room and shadows moved across the screen.

"Why do you think she prefers Sam?" Zed was still thinking about Sarah. We'd both seen her in the stairwell, on our way back up, sucking your face as if she could draw life from it. You were entwined like vines wrapped around a tree, her perfectly tanned leg looped over your hip, leaning into you for support, her brown hair fanning across your face like a blanket, shielding you from Zed's look of disgust.

"It's because I'm Chinese." Zed drained his beer. His heart-shaped face seemed to be getting smaller, and his eyes were turned down at the corners, droopy with fatigue and alcohol.

"You don't know that." An image of Rob surrounded by blondes in tight shirts, as if he were the last man on earth, flashed through my mind. Suddenly, I felt angry at Zed for crying about what we couldn't have. Why did Sarah matter so much? With her square jaw, long nose, and small lips, she wasn't even the best-looking girl there. She was just another Art History major from a nice Chicago suburb biding her time until Mr. Right found her.

"Jesus, Zed. What were you expecting? What's changed since last week?"

"I thought the party would be small."

"That you were special for being invited."

He said nothing.

"Amelia wasn't invited," I said. Amelia, who wouldn't have come anyway because she always helped her parents on Friday nights when their restaurant got so packed, there'd be a line spilling over into Little Italy one block down.

"Too chinky," he said.

"Don't say that."

"You know that's what they see—little China girl, with her plaits and bow-legs."

"Just don't say it. It sounds like that's how you see her."

He was silent.

"Do you?" Suddenly I needed to know. "Do you?"

"I don't." But he hesitated. "I don't know."

The silence lay there between us, a break in the smooth surface of our friendship, like the crack in the mahogany coffee table he once found on the street for me. I stood up, and the tar beneath my feet sank a bit, still soft from baking in the summer sun. The paper lanterns strung across the roof swayed in the breeze, and the smell of fried fish wafted up from the alley.

"Want a drink?"

I knew what I was doing. I knew I was walking away, leaving the ghost of the words between us. It was as if he'd told me he had herpes. I didn't want to know.

"Beer," he said, holding up his cup without looking at me. His shoulders were hunched, and the cup shook slightly in his hand.

That was his last word to me. From another person, this might be remembered as funny, a wry commentary on who he was. But beer was about who Zed wanted to be, the kind of guy girls like Sarah would wrap themselves around, not the Chinese-American geek who never told me his real name, only that he'd changed it, gone straight to Zed, the last stop in the alphabet.

Zed understood something about the two of us, but I had put my hands over my ears and eyes and didn't want to know. When I went downstairs for my refills—so urgent, so necessary, as if more of anything let alone beer could fill me up—I would not think of him earlier handing me the beer with the least foam or the way he placed a protective hand on my back and helped guide me through the crowd. I wouldn't remember any of that because there was Rob, sitting in one of the bedrooms, smoking a cigarette alone. He beckoned to me, and if I thought about Zed, it was only for a second.

"I've been waiting for you," Rob said. "Where d'you go off to?"

The lampshade was covered with silk scarves, and in the dim light, his voice sounded deeper, richer, huskier than it had in the crowded hallway. I approached him and let him take the cups from my hands. He patted the platform bed, and I sat down.

"I have to take them to the roof. Zed's waiting."

"Who?"

I started to explain, but he got up. I thought he was leaving. I looked down at the floor, studied the grain of the stained oak.

I heard the door close and felt the mattress sink as he sat down again. I smelled tobacco, beer, and sweat, and then I heard the thumping as people in the living room danced to a favorite college song, one that prompted synchronized yelling every other minute. I don't want to remember anything else, tell you that when Rob kissed me, I wasn't thinking of Zed and when I felt his arms around me, his hands on my skin, his tongue on my neck, I didn't think, this man doesn't even know my name. I didn't think, I have a friend waiting for me upstairs on a dark roof looking into someone else's apartment for company, waiting and perhaps wondering if he needs to rescue me. I didn't think, okay? I can't even say I gave Rob much thought; my loneliness was a deep, hidden ache that came alive and fell to its knees with a certain touch.

I know those two girls, the students in your homeroom who you expected so much and so little from. I have known them all my life. They are the girls and boys who write down every assignment, cross them off a list that includes extra homework, assigned by their language teacher—Mandarin, Cantonese, Hindi, Urdu—the one they sit with after school while all the other kids play outside. They have plenty of time, always have time for homework.

Their parents do not allow them to go to school dances, or if they go, they are picked up and brought home early, long before they can be invited to the after-party at Michael's or Susan's house, where there will be beer, cigarettes, pot, but mostly kissing and groping in the dark shadows of an unfamiliar living room where the upholstery and carpeting match, just like they do in the magazines.

These kids do not get invited to parties because they are not around, and soon no one remembers to miss them, so even when they are around, no one sees them. At home, their parents tell them the only thing that matters is hard work; sports exist only to make you a better student and get you into the right school. Fun is an American habit, and they are not American, at least not in that way.

And at school, their heads drop a little, they struggle to hang in there, grateful for their good grades, confused by your puzzled smile when you hand back another perfect quiz, as if to say, don't you ever fuck up?

Later, when I left the bedroom, I realized all the lights were on, the apartment was quiet, and it was completely empty. Plastic cups, overflowing ashtrays, and streamers littered the living room, and crushed popcorn covered Sarah's grandmother's Persian rug. I looked at the blinking light on the VCR; past midnight, and I didn't know how long it had been since I had left Zed with the promise of refills I no longer had. I wondered if he'd come looking for me, had been that knock on the door I fuzzily remembered now. My mouth was dry, and I smelled unlike myself, like a stranger had taken up residence in my skin.

Then Sarah, tear-stained and heavy-footed like a lame horse, stomped into the apartment. Her roommates and some of our friends followed her and a policeman with bright red hair, not much older than us, looking stern but otherwise unmoved by the sight of tears and the sounds of sniffing and an occasional sob.

I knew. I knew because the ache I kept so tightly contained had flowered like an ink stain on tissue paper, a permanent tattoo of grief, with the heart-shaped face and thick black hair of the boy I loved so incompletely. Etched in indigo, rimmed in red, filled with purple bruises, that ache has one name.

You want to know about him, so many years too late, and I can only tell you about me because I'm still here. Afterwards, I let the rest of you claim him; Sarah called his parents, but two weeks later, at the memorial service she organized, they finally remembered me, asked me, "Where were you?" And at work, Amelia said, "Why didn't you stop him?"

She was the only one. No one else imagined that he could have been stopped. The story we told ourselves went like this: he'd had too much to drink, hadn't seen the gap in the ledge, it was too dark and he backed over it, fell into the alley six storeys below, leaving his imprint in the garbage and dirt, flattening a cardboard box that might or might not have been someone's home. The cardboard box, that was the closest we got to the truth.

I lost weight. My jeans hung at my hips and everyone thought that my mourning was eating my body from the inside out, consuming me bit by bit and one day I would disappear, go right over the edge.

I was already gone. I didn't tell anyone that every night I was listening to the phone, replaying the answering machine to make sure I hadn't missed Rob's message. I willed myself to ignore the phone, hid it under pillows, under the couch, under piles of dirty laundry that sat like small wrinkled mountains around my bed, and still I found myself picking up the receiver, making sure it hadn't gone dead.

I replayed it again and again, an endless loop of images that filled me with shame, made me desperate: the creaking floorboard, the sour-sweet smell of stale beer and sweat and the rough edge of uneven teeth under the tip of my tongue.

Later, I would stare at the phone, imagining I had missed the call only minutes before coming through the door.

The bones around the base of my neck were sticking out. At work, Amelia pulled me into the bathroom and said, "Stop it. Starving yourself to death won't bring him back."

I looked down at the hexagon tiles, cracked around the base of the sink, and longed to slip between them, become part of this floor where each and every tile started out looking exactly alike, with exactly the same chance of being cracked or staying intact as they aged. How could I tell her? That even in his death, I valued Zed less than a casual fuck in a strange bed.

Why do some girls lay themselves down on the train tracks, give themselves over to a certain death, while their sisters and brothers find a way to go on? I don't know.

I have felt Zed's hand on my shoulder, holding me back from the ledge. He did for me what I couldn't do for him or myself. In the long dark nights I spent looking out my window, waiting for the pink and gray streaks of daybreak, he reminded me my life was not worthless.

And one day, I came home, ate dinner, read the paper, picked up my dirty clothes, and around bed time I realized I hadn't looked at the phone, had forgotten to look for the blinking light of messages. I had none, and this fact did not bother me. Finally, I was left with this: a TV flickering in the dark. A sultry summer evening. A ledge with a gap I never saw. A hole in my heart so big you could fall all the way to China. Or at least Hong Kong.

That's what Zed used to say every time someone broke his heart.

I'll tell you. Those two girls who lay down on the tracks together. I know them. I know they worked hard in school and became best friends because there was no one else for them. I know their parents, well-meaning, anxious people who think the answer lies in books, and friends and fun and parties are for Americans, not people like us.

Understand, I have chosen to go on living, but when I saw them in the paper this morning, two gray girls entombed in newsprint, when I looked in their faces, they looked like Zed and me. Ten years later. You were there, with your sun-streaked hair and confident smile, looking like you'd stepped out of the pages of a glossy fashion magazine. You know what happened. So what am I telling you that you don't already know? But maybe you didn't notice us on the beer-soaked stairwell, your face buried in Sarah's neck, Sarah, who would dump you after the memorial, after you decided to give up banking and become a teacher, of all things. I heard you said that a life lived for others wasn't a life at all. And still, all the training, role-playing, in-service days in the world couldn't have prepared you for this, the day the principal would come in and tell you that two girls from your class were dead. That's why you called. You wonder if you are to blame.

You want me to tell you about these foreign faces filling your classroom, with their afterschool language classes and their parents who talk about home as another country, these boys and girls who cluster together when they can, and when they can't, hug the walls at recess, a familiar longing in their faces as they watch their classmates play.

I'm thinking about tiles. Who can predict those unseen pressures that make some tiles crack and leave others seemingly intact? Sometimes the whole ones, the perfect smooth ones that still look new, sometimes those are the first to go. One day you'll be looking down at the floor and where there was a tile, there is now a gaping hole, a hexagon or a square, you notice this for the first time. It popped right up and disappeared. Yet the cracked ones, they too are troubled but something holds them in place, makes them fit even when they are not quite right, have never been right, from the first time they were laid.

I have no answers for you, I can't make things all right. That's the thing about tiles, Sam. You can never tell and by the time you can, it's too late.

# Dharma Farm

Gus Kuthiala dragged his sister down the aisle of the bus. Her clammy hand curled into a fist, and he struggled to hold on to it. They were on their way to a specialty pet store on Second Avenue to buy a birthday present for their brother-in-law. Gus knew Nikita wanted to exit at the front of the bus, but this was New York, not Pittsburgh, and here you got off the bus at the back. Common sense: you paid and moved to the back, so you got off at the back.

For a doctor, Nikita didn't have much common sense.

Nikita pulled her hand out of his. She was small and thin, with short black hair and narrow shoulders. From behind she looked like a child not a grown woman of twenty-seven.

"You're not the boss of me," she said.

"Our stop's next."

The bus lurched forward and a siren screamed past, followed by the screech of tires and the louder, more insistent clang and wail of a fire truck. Gus's sneakers stuck to the floor of the bus. The smell of grape juice wafted up mingled with the smell of peppermint soap emanating from one of the other passengers. Gus squeezed past a man in a white shirt and black pants hanging on a strap.

Gus kept moving. An old woman with a shopping bag in her lap leaned into a younger woman in a white uniform sitting next to her. The young woman huffed and resettled her large frame in the seat. She had long purple fingernails with tiny rhinestones glued to them. Gus turned around. A gangly teenager with ear buds in his big ears stood between him and Nikita. The teenager's large backpack blocked the space between them.

"Nurse's assistant," Gus mouthed and jerked his head towards the purple fingernails.

Nikita frowned at the teenager's backpack, which was a couple of inches from her nose. Gus wiped the sweat from his forehead. Why had he agreed to Nikita's plan? Sharmila had warned him that she was unpredictable. Childhood was a distant memory for Gus, but Sharmila remembered each and every one of Nikita's fits.

"Fits?" Gus wanted to know what he had missed.

"Trust me," Shar said. "She's a bomb waiting to go off."

The bus still wasn't moving. The store was on 35th Street, between a diner and a hair salon that sold shoes. The bus stop was on 34th, and they were stuck at the light, where crosstown traffic blocked the intersection.

"We should have got off at 36th," Nikita said.

The bus was hot, the air conditioning ineffective with so many bodies pressed together. Nikita wiped her neck with her hand. She had refused to grow her hair long for Sharmila's wedding last year, claiming a big head of hair would interfere with her work. Gus had standing orders to cut his before family gatherings, but this was the band's best season yet. No way was he going to cut his hair. Dharma Farm was in its second incarnation, and this line up was better than the first. It was only a matter of time before they had enough material for an album. Last week, they'd played the Rodeo to a packed house. Gus's hair was one of his best features, even though right now it felt like a small kitten on the back of his neck.

"Excuse me," Nikita said to the backpack.

The boy ignored her.

"Would you please move?"

Then, before Gus could stop her, Nikita extended her finger and poked the boy in the shoulder.

"What the fuck," the boy turned around, slamming Gus in the chest with his backpack.

"You're blocking the aisle," Nikita said.

The bus started moving suddenly, and the boy fell against Gus. Nikita pushed past him, and then the bus stopped again, and before Gus could say or do anything, she was through the back door and standing on the street, waiting for him.

They'd met at her hotel uptown. She'd been at a conference all morning, and the late afternoon was the only time they had before heading out to Jersey for their brother-in-law's birthday party. It was going to be at a hotel, catered, with a DJ. Sharmila had planned it all, a surprise for her new husband.

"Mom told me to tell you to get your hair cut."

Nikita was sitting at the bar in the hotel, drinking orange juice. She looked—there was no other word for it—pressed. Her white blouse was well cut, her red cotton skirt flared gently at the knee, and she was wearing summer sandals with a small heel. Gus was used to seeing her in scrubs or jeans. She did not look like a harried ER doctor from Pittsburgh. She looked European.

Gus grabbed her juice and drained it. He was dehydrated, had been up late the night before, practicing at a warehouse on the west side.

"I'm not sure about this."

"You're just annoyed because Shar didn't want your band to play."

Gus grabbed her wrist and looked at her Swiss Army watch. He did not wear a watch, nor did he carry a cell phone. The more his mother insisted on the phone—even offering to pay for his iPhone—the less inclined he was to carry one.

Nikita pulled her wrist back. "I don't know why you didn't let me just meet you there."

"Sisters are your dharma, Gus." His mother never missed an opportunity to remind him. "You're the oldest. You're a boy."

When he asked for an explanation of dharma, his mother had been typically vague, as if the understanding was part of his genetic code. She referred him to the Bhagavad Gita, our holy book, beta and told him to read Krishna's speech to Arjuna, just before he went into battle. What Gus really needed was a comic book explanation, not the source, but his mother made no concessions for her American children. She gave him an old translation and that was that.

"You'd be lost," Gus said. "Don't even deny it."

Nikita had no sense of direction, and she didn't like Manhattan. She wasn't, therefore, a girl to be trusted on public transportation. When they were little and used to come into the city to go to the theatre or museums, Nikita clung to their mother's hand and cried. Perhaps these were the "fits" Sharmila remembered.

"I could have taken a taxi," she said, looking into her glass like she could use more juice. She signaled to the waiter, who was at a table, tending to a bunch of suits.

"Forget the juice," Gus said. "We have to be there in a couple of hours." The party started at eight, but guests had to be there by 7:30.

She didn't want to go to the party any more than he did; Sharmila's husband, Neil, worked for the NBA and acted like he was one cool desi because he'd avoided becoming a doctor or an engineer. He was an accountant and a perfect match for Sharmila who, like Nikita, was a doctor. Unlike Nikita, however, Sharmila wanted nothing to do with sick people. She'd chosen dermatology and worked for one of those cosmetic centers, overseeing laser hair removal. "Don't screw this up," Sharmila had said to Gus last month. "His whole family is going to be there."

"How would we screw it up?" Gus asked.

Sharmila jerked her head towards Nikita, who was out of earshot. "Drama. It travels with her, like hotel soap or shampoo in those tiny bottles."

The two girls, with ten months between them, might as well have been a generation apart. Sharmila resented Nikita for being planned, four years after Gus, and Nikita resented Sharmila for stealing her place as the baby. "Take care of your sisters," his mother said, when she called from work. "Don't let them fight."

After hanging up the phone, he'd put his headphones back on and listen to the stereo while watching TV without the sound, until one of the girls came running into the living room. Neither of them actually wanted a solution, he concluded. They liked to fight.

Now he grabbed Nikita's arm and pulled her away from the bar.

"This was your idea. Let's do it."

• • •

The store was a dark shadow, with no sign, just a window where two bichon puppies played in a pile of shredded paper. Nikita stopped and stared at them.

"Come on," Gus said. He pulled the door open. The store closed at five; they had fifteen minutes.

"Forget it," Nikita said.

Gus paused in the threshold, let out a blast of cold air. It smelled of wet grass and disinfectant.

"You're the one who said geckoes would be cute. Original."

He hated geckoes. He'd been thinking this, sitting on a sofa in New Delhi one summer, half listening to his parents and grandparents talk in their usual mix of Punjabi, Hindi, and English, when a gecko fell from the ceiling. It landed in his hair, which was thick and curly then. For hours, he couldn't stop shaking his head, feeling imaginary toe pads on his scalp. His grandfather used the incident to drag him to a barber. He said a good haircut would keep the geckoes out.

Nikita thought geckoes would make a good present for Neil, who liked tropical fish. "If we're not original, Shar will think we don't care."

"We don't," Gus said.

Someone inside the store said, "Hey. I'm not paying to air condition the city. In or out, buddy. In or out."

Gus shut the door and stepped onto the street. His t-shirt was sticking to his back. The sensible thing to do right now would be to go to Macy's and buy Neil some nose hair clippers or a foot massager. Gus grabbed his sister's arm. The fabric of her shirt felt tissue paper thin, and he was surprised by the hard curve of the muscle underneath it.

She let him pull her into the store. Inside, the black and white linoleum floor was dirty and chipped. Fish tanks lined the wall to Gus's left, back lit and calm, and bags of pet food and random dog toys lay piled near the door. The room smelled of mold and damp, of green furry stuff growing in dark corners. At the back, illuminated by bright overhead fluorescent lights stood a man. He was behind the counter, with a newspaper folded in his left hand, a pen in his right. He appeared to be concentrating on the crossword puzzle while talking to himself.

"No. Yes. She didn't tell me."

His face was pale and round, like the moon, and his belly strained against his maroon shirt. He put his hand to his right ear, where a Bluetooth glowed like a phosphorescent growth.

"Gotta go," he said. He pulled the phone out of his ear and put it in a drawer.

Gus nudged Nikita forward. This was her party. He went to stand by the glass windows to his right, cages set into the wall. There were four, big and bright. In one, two daschunds slept, curled into each other, tiny and fetal. Next to them, two tabbies played with a cat tree, oblivious to their human audience. Below them, a bichon yipped and wagged its fluffy little tail. The word "SOLD" appeared in red letters on a tag in the corner of all three cages.

In the last cage, a black dog lay on the mesh platform, filling the entire cage with its furry mass. Forty or fifty pounds, eyes closed. There was no tag in the corner.

"The Humane Society has a hotline," Nikita said.

The man looked at Gus. "Most of these cats and dogs will be gone by next week. After that, it's strictly fish and reptiles."

"What about geckoes?" Gus asked.

Nikita had pulled out her cell phone. First it was the kid on the bus, now this hapless guy trying to finish the crossword. Gus thought about what he'd tell Sharmila when they arrived late, censored all of it, and took his sister's arm.

"For the last and final time, Gus, you are not the boss of me."

When she and Sharmila fought, Nikita was always right. She could not back down, and Gus had to sit between the sisters—with his headphones—until Sharmila apologized. The peace between them was fragile, prone to breaking with one wrong move. At Sharmila's wedding, it had been Nikita flirting with Neil's best man that provoked Shar to say, "Stop acting like a slut. You're ruining my wedding." Nikita did what she wanted, when she wanted. Any filter she had seemed only to exist when she was at work. Out in the world, she was deceptive—well dressed, short and delicate, she did not look like someone with steel in her biceps. She did not look like someone who would poke a kid on the bus.

The man at the cash register looked at Gus.

"Sister?"

Gus shrugged.

"I have three," the man said. "And thanks to technology, I can listen to them any time of the day."

"How about geckoes? You have any of those?"

"Next week. After the kittens go."

The black puppy was sitting up in the cage, its head bent forward. "What about that one?" Gus said.

The man left the counter and stood beside him by the cages, breathing heavily. "Geckoes bite. Aggressive bastards." He sneezed and blew his nose. Then he opened a door hidden in the wall, disappeared and came back with the puppy on a leash.

"Newfs are hard in this neighborhood. People look at their paws, they see problems."

The dog sat; its paws were like platters. Gus held out his hand, and the dog licked it enthusiastically, stood up and wagged its tail. Puppies were so easy to please. Unlike sisters.

"I'll give you a hundred," Gus said. He'd just been paid. A shoot out at Astoria yesterday, a pudding commercial. The money was in his wallet, for the geckoes. He'd wanted to surprise Nikita, pay his share, show her he was financially viable. About his chosen profession, she and Sharmila had agreed; if they waited long enough, he'd outgrow the band and become a man they could introduce their friends to. As an older brother, he was an embarrassment. Calling the band Dharma Farm only compounded the problem.

"Are you saying the farm is where people live out their karmic duty?" Sharmila said.

"Don't be so literal," Gus said.

"It sounds like something a dumb American would come up with," Nikita said.

This was five years ago, when Gus made his resolution about cell phones. He did not need his sisters in his ear.

The man handed the leash to Gus.

Nikita walked to the front of the store, her phone against her ear. The owner disappeared behind the door again.

"Earth First too busy to take your call?" Gus said. The puppy pressed into his legs.

"It's the Humane Society, you idiot."

The owner returned carrying two metal bowls. "I call her Sophie. But you can change her name."

Sophie wagged her butt and smiled. Her teeth were white, her tongue a pink waterfall.

Nikita took the leash from Gus's hand and gave it back to the owner. "You can't buy a dog at a pet store."

Gus took the leash back. "You're not the boss of me," he said, but his heart wasn't in it. When would he walk a dog? He didn't even know if his building allowed dogs.

"Mom will have a fit if we show up with a dog."

"We can give it to Neil." A puppy was cuter than a gecko. And still original.

The door to the store opened, and a tall woman with a big straw hat swept in. She took off her oversized sunglasses and glared at Gus and Nikita. Sophie barked and pulled at her leash.

"Harry, you jerk. I told you I was coming back for her."

"Gina, you either want it or you don't. In or out. You can't keep a dog in a cage forever."

"I told ma you'd do this." She was young, her brown hair hung straight down her back, and several gold rings flashed on her long, elegant fingers. She was wearing a sleeveless black dress, cinched at the waist, and the kind of leather sandals that barely covered her feet. She was as unlike the slob behind the counter as geckoes were from the puppy. "Sophie, come."

The dog jumped, taking Gus by surprise, and before he could stop her she had her paws up on Gina's legs, and Gina was kneeling and accepting her enthusiastic kisses.

Nikita crossed her arms. "We just paid for this dog."

"Give the people their money," Gina said to her brother.

Harry crossed his arms.

"Your dog, your money."

"One hundred," Nikita said.

Gina opened her wallet and started counting bills.

"You said you didn't have any money," Harry said.

Gina ignored him.

"We're going to be late," Gus said.

Gina looked at him. "I know you from somewhere."

"Dharma Farm. We played the Rodeo last week." Gus couldn't believe it. An actual fan.

"I don't listen to live music," Gina said. She gave Gus five twenties.

"If you give me your email, I'll put you on our mailing list." Gus patted his back pocket for a card. She was cute when she wasn't scowling. No piercings, no visible tattoos.

"I'm not running a kennel," Harry said.

"You have a brother?" Gina asked Nikita.

Nikita pointed at Gus.

"Then you know how it goes. You ask him to do you a favor—while you're moving apartments, so your puppy, who's been living with you for a month, won't be freaked out. But he's too busy doing crosswords to make his business work, so first offer he gets on your dog, your dog that you bought at a breeder because only an asshole buys dogs at a pet store, he gives her up." She looked at her brother, her eyes blazing. "My own brother."

"We just wanted a birthday present," Gus said.

"Geckoes are not good gifts," Harry said. "They're moody and unforgiving."

"The perfect gift," Gus said. "If you don't like the person you're giving them to."

"Hey," Nikita said.

"I'm on to you," Gus said. There was no love lost between his sisters; why spare any for Neil, the wonder boy? "You want to see Neil's face when that gecko bites him."

Nikita bent down, and Sophie sniffed and licked her face. She ran her hands over the dog's body, and the dog lay down on her back, exposing a white belly.

"It's not fair," Nikita said, her voice muffled.

Gus knelt next to Nikita, but she would not look at him.

"Why can't you just be happy for her? She's your sister."

"You don't understand," Nikita said.

"Sisters are worse than brothers," Gina said.

"True," Harry said.

*Take care of your sisters.*

When the priest at the temple had talked about dharma, Gus was reading a comic book. When he talked about vocation, Gus was drumming his thigh, replaying the rhythms of the tape he'd been listening to that morning. When the priest talked, when his sisters fought, when his mother called from work and told him to start dinner, Gus's mind had been elsewhere.

Sharmila and Nikita had their dharma. But what was his? Over thirty, still playing in a band, Gus couldn't take care of his sisters in any practical way. He couldn't even sit between them anymore. At the table of life, he'd be placed at the kiddie table.

"We should have gone to Macy's," he said.

## Acknowledgments

I am indebted to my colleagues and fellow students at the *Kenyon Review* Writers' Workshop, especially Anna Duke Reach, David Lynn, Ron Carlson and Nancy Zafris. Without Nancy, this collection would not exist. I'm also grateful to Kit Irwin and Nicola Dixon who influenced many of these stories.

Thanks to the Pennsylvania Council on the Arts, the Ragdale Foundation, Eastern Frontier Society, the Vira I. Heinz Foundation, and the Virginia Center for Creative Arts.

Special thanks to Kathleen Lee and Kristin Cosby, who read closely and carefully, and to Sandy Foster, who makes my day job manageable.

I'm indebted to Jeff Oaks and Jenny Johnson, who keep me focused.

For encouragement and support, I'm grateful to my friends and family: Jane McCafferty, Bill Lychack and Chauna Craig; Sherill Tippins and Bob Mecoy; Jean Grace, Amy Twyning, and Juli Parrish; Judy Vollmer, Amrita Puri, Karen Woodall, Rachel Brickner, Peter Kusnic, Robert Stevens, Sejal Shah, Parul Kapur Hinzen, Sangamithra Iyer, and Minal Hajratwala; Meera Kothari, Glenn Cho, and Kelly Woodward.

Jim Francis read every single word in this collection multiple times and with far more patience than I deserved. To him and ADF, a big hug (just kidding).

Mark Kemp brings me tea every morning, makes me laugh, and rewrites my bad sentences. *Thank you* doesn't even begin to cover it.

Geeta Kothari is the nonfiction editor of the *Kenyon Review*. She is a co-founder of the www.novelworkshop.org. Her writing has appeared in various anthologies and journals, including *New England Review, Massachusetts Review*, and others. Her essay "If You Are What You Eat, Then What Am I?" is widely taught in universities and has been reprinted in several anthologies, including in *Best American Essays*. She is the editor of *Did My Mama Like to Dance?: And Other Stories about Mothers and Daughters.*

CPSIA information can be obtained
at www.ICGtesting.com
Printed in the USA
FFOW02n1231030417
34108FF